Saskia's Journey

THERESA BRESLIN

CORGI BOOKS

SASKIA'S JOURNEY
A CORGI BOOK 0 552 54865 0

First published in Great Britain by Doubleday,
an imprint of Random House Children's Books

Doubleday edition published 2004
Corgi edition published 2005

5 7 9 10 8 6

Papers used by Random House Children's Books are natural,
recyclable products made from wood grown in sustainable forests.
The manufacturing processes conform to the environmental
regulations of the country of origin.

Corgi Books are published by Random House Children's Books,
61–63 Uxbridge Road, London W5 5SA,
a division of The Random House Group Ltd,
in Australia by Random House Australia (Pty) Ltd,
20 Alfred Street, Milsons Point, Sydney, NSW 2061, Australia,
in New Zealand by Random House New Zealand Ltd,
18 Poland Road, Glenfield, Auckland 10, New Zealand,
and in South Africa by Random House (Pty) Ltd,
Endulini, 5A Jubilee Road, Parktown 2193, South Africa

THE RANDOM HOUSE GROUP Limited Reg. No. 954009
www.**kids**at**randomhouse**.co.uk

A CIP catalogue record for this book is available from the British
Library.

The Random House Group Limited supports The Forest Stewardship
Council (FSC®), the leading international forest certification organisation.
Our books carrying the FSC label are printed on FSC® certified paper.
FSC is the only forest certification scheme endorsed by the leading
environmental organisations, including Greenpeace. Our
paper procurement policy can be found at
www.randomhouse.co.uk/environment

Printed and bound in Great Britain by Clays Ltd, St Ives PLC

For the people of the lands
of Buchan

With special thanks to
Ann and Bert

DEAD RECKONING – a method of establishing one's position using the distance and direction travelled rather than astronomical observations.

Muckle Flugga

Sumburgh Head

Brough of Birsay

Butt of Lewis   Cape Wrath

Flannan Isles   Pentland Skerries

Buckie harbour
Kinnaird Head
Fraserburgh Harbour
Buchan Ness

Ardnamurchan   Tod Head

Skerryvore   Bell Rock

Methil Outer Pier   Isle of May

Rhinns of Islay

Farne Islands

Souter, Newcastle-Upon-Tyne

Mull of Galloway   Whitby High

The Skerries   Spurn Point

Trwyn-du

Lowestoft
Southwold

Strumble Head

Lundy

Dungeness

The
Needles

Wolf Rock   Eddystone

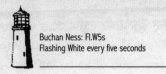

Buchan Ness: Fl.W5s
Flashing White every five seconds

Chapter 1

And now Saskia was aware of the sea.

Glancing up from her book, it filled her vision at once and so completely that she drew in her breath. Without thinking she reached out her hand so that her fingers touched the train window, and the tension of the last weeks sloughed from her mind as she gave way to a familiar response of wonder and delight. Childhood memories surfaced – school trips to the seaside, long happy days playing on the beach, watching the waves; and Saskia knew that she was smiling.

The sea had little thought for Saskia.

It was the time of the spawning. From the Davis Strait to the Barents Sea, and beyond Rockall and Malin towards the Hebrides and the Shetlands, the shoals were moving in from deep water. Round Cape Wrath, the Butt of Lewis and the Faeroe Isles, silent streams of fish, pelagic and demersal, sought out their breeding grounds . . .

Saskia tucked her book into her rucksack and leaned her

forehead on the window glass. She would never tire of looking at the sea. The variety of its moods bewitched her as did the sensation of being caught up in light and space between her own self and the unreachable horizon.

In the days when her parents had seemed interested in what she thought and her home was a less dangerous place to be, she had struggled with the mind of a child to explain a concept that she couldn't grasp. She had been nine or ten and crying at the end of a summer's day spent by the sea when it came time for them to drive home to the city once more.

'Why?' her parents had asked her. 'Why do you like the sea so much?'

'There's nothing like it. It's always changing and it . . . it doesn't end . . . anywhere.' Saskia had spread her hands out wide and then up and down to illustrate her idea of infinite dimensions.

Now she glimpsed the North Sea from time to time beyond the line of the houses that rimmed the shore as the train slipped through a changing vista of mountain and valley. Fingers of spring were uncurling winter's fist from the land – yellow broom and golden gorse thrusting through on the lower ground, the tops of the far hills still shawled in snow. Often the train was only metres away from the water's edge then abruptly the line would twist inland to run through wooded areas and little towns.

From when she was quite young Saskia had known that she wanted to learn more about the ocean; that playing sandcastles and even graduating to surfing and sailing was not enough. As she grew older, on days out she begged to be taken to aquariums or Sea World centres. She would stand for hours with her face close against the reinforced glass staring at the marine life. Once, it happened that she was suddenly conscious of her size compared to the fish within the tank; of how her great eye, magnified by the glass, might appear to the other living thing watching her. She felt a surge of power then and deliberately widened her eye with the conscious cruelty of a child seeking to terrify a smaller creature. Unimpressed, the fish gaped at her, flicked its tail and swam away.

She was always drawn to the more unusual specimens, some mere pale ghosts of mucous jelly. The sight of these with their blindly waving translucent tendrils repelled her mother, who would shudder and call them sinister.

Sinister.

Interesting why that particular word should enter her mind at this moment. Was it because it best described the household she had left or the one she was going to? The only photograph she had ever seen of her great-aunt Alessandra showed a thin woman, standing alone, hands clasped in front of her, unsmiling, before a house of grey granite. Saskia had not been attracted to this relative whom her father had encouraged her to visit.

'Be especially nice to her, pet, won't you?' Her father draped his arm around her shoulder. 'Your great-aunt Alessandra has written and asked particularly for you to come. And I think now it's time you saw her again.'

At first Saskia had resisted – the place was so far away – but she found it difficult to refuse her dad when he was on one of his charm offensives.

'There are lots of coastal paths there. Why don't you take your bicycle with you and explore the area? The house is right next to the sea so you could look at shells and, and . . . erm . . . other things.' He grinned and winked, and she was so glad to be having his attention that she mentally sidestepped the realization that he didn't actually appreciate how much she still loved the sea, and that her interest was more than collecting pretty shells.

Eventually Saskia had relented and agreed to take some time out in her gap year to spend two weeks with her father's aunt Alessandra. 'You'll find Alessandra an odd old biddy,' her dad had said.

'Not so old,' her mother had interrupted.

Saskia's dad continued as though his wife had not spoken. 'A strange old spinster woman in a strange old house. A house full of secrets.' He laughed. 'Rumour is that there's some fortune stashed away in that mausoleum she lives in. My father was her older brother. There were just the two of them so we are her only living relatives. You be really attentive to her and perhaps we can wheedle a little legacy in advance. Better us to have it than it buried with her.' He pulled Saskia closer for a hug. 'We could put it to good use, couldn't we? Go on a spending spree together? It would make life easier for all of us.'

'Not *us*,' her mother had said distinctly. 'Not Saskia and me. Not us. *You*.'

'Now, darling' – Saskia's father's voice purred soft and warm in her hair as he replied to her mother – 'let's not forget how good you are at spending money. It's one of the few skills you possess.'

As he spoke her father let his arm drop and stepped back to look at his wife. And in that moment the look that came and went between her parents was both terrible and indescribable so that Saskia shook. She shivered in the train then, although it wasn't cold.

At Aberdeen station Saskia collected her bicycle and rucksack and walked along the platform with the rest of the passengers. She paused at the station exit, saw a man standing smoking beside an old pick-up truck lift his head and look at her carefully. He nicked out his cigarette with his thumb and forefinger and dropped the stub end into his pocket as he came forward to meet her.

'Saskia Granton.' It was a statement rather than a question.

Saskia nodded.

'I'm Neil, Neil Buchan, the taxi driver. Miss Alessandra Granton sent me to fetch ye. She said ye'd have a bike wi' ye, so I brought the pick-up instead of my car.'

Saskia smiled, and to make conversation said, 'I'm surprised you recognized me so quickly among all these people.'

The man opened the door of the pick-up for her. 'A'body would ken yer face. Yer like the woman herself right enough.'

And as Saskia climbed into the passenger seat she heard him add under his breath as he closed the door, 'God help ye.'

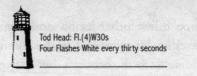

Tod Head: Fl.(4)W30s
Four Flashes White every thirty seconds

Chapter 2

'There.' Neil Buchan took one hand from the steering wheel and pointed ahead. 'If ye look there ye'll see the Granton house when we get round the top of this hill.'

Saskia's legs were cramped and she struggled to sit upright as the truck turned the bend in the road. 'Oh!' she said. 'Oh, my goodness!'

'Aye, it's quite a sicht.' Neil pulled the truck across to the other side of the road and onto the grass verge.

Saskia wound down the window. Immediately the sound and the smell of the sea filled her senses. She pulled open the door, jumped down from the pick-up truck and walked across the stubble grass to the barrier fence almost at the cliff edge.

Neil came and stood beside her. 'Tak' care,' he said. 'This bit of headland is apt to crumble.'

They were standing above the southern point of a small smoothly curved indent of land. High cliffs stood back from the narrow strip of beach and at the further end, halfway down the cliff, was a three-storey house with its back set into the rock face. There was a tiny square of garden to the left-hand side and then an almost vertical drop to the beach below. Saskia could see stairs carved into the cliff which led to the beach.

'I wouldn't have thought it possible to have a house there!' she exclaimed.

'A lot of the older houses on this stretch of coast were built like that. The land falls away so steeply that ye reach the top level by outside stairs. The space below the roof was used to store the fishing nets. But that house is certainly special. This is the only point on the road that ye can see it. From anywhere else ye wouldna' ken it was there.'

Granite stone glittered on the walls of the house shouldered into the cliff, the quartz catching the light reflected by the sun going down behind the hills on the western horizon. The windows appeared sightless, but then that wasn't true, thought Saskia. The sun's rays glancing on the window glass meant that she couldn't see in, not that someone inside couldn't see out. The reverse in fact. On an evening like this a person inside the house could watch the road without being seen. Was her great-aunt watching for her? Saskia gazed at the house and it returned her stare.

Saskia breathed in deeply to clear her head. It had been a very long train journey north from London, and almost another hour or so in the pick-up, but despite her tiredness the imminent presence of the sea had raised her spirits. She climbed back into the cab.

'We have to leave the truck here,' Neil said a few minutes later as he slowed down and drew into an opening at the right-hand side of the road. 'We walk down to your aunt's house by this path. Look ye now,' he added, as he lifted Saskia's rucksack and left her to wheel her bicycle, 'the nearest village, Fhindhaven, is round the next bend o' the road, less than a ten-minute walk, and there's a bus passes this way every hour, north to Inverness, south to Aberdeen. And' – he paused – 'my house is the first one ye come to on the top road into the village, the one with the red roof. There's a'ways somebody about if ye need any help.'

Help.

The word lodged in Saskia's mind as she followed Neil Buchan down the steep path to her great-aunt's house.

Great-aunt Alessandra was waiting for her, standing in the frame of the door at the gable end of the house. Saskia saw her step down onto the path and then stop, to wait for Saskia to come to her.

Alessandra Granton was considerably younger than Saskia had expected her to be. She recalled her mother's words, describing Alessandra. 'Not so old', she had said, but her father had spoken of his aunt as though she were ninety. Saskia did some quick mental arithmetic. She knew that her grandfather and great-grandfather had died at sea just after the Second World War, first one, then the other, only a year or so later. Her grandfather, her father's father, had been just twenty years old and Alessandra was his younger sister. This being 1988, her great-aunt could only be in her fifties. This woman's face, although lined around the eyes, was smoothly composed. Her hair was pulled back into a knot, twisted and held at the nape of her neck. She held her hands in front of her, just as in the photograph that Saskia had seen,

8

fingers of one hand clasped around the wrist of the other.

Only when Saskia was quite close to her did Alessandra offer a greeting.

'Welcome, Saskia. Welcome to Cliff House.'

Saskia shook her great-aunt's outstretched hand. 'Thank you for having me to stay, Great-aunt Alessandra.'

To Saskia's surprise her great-aunt's face flushed. Alessandra didn't reply, only hurried past Saskia to take the bicycle from Neil Buchan.

'Let me do that for ye,' he said.

'No,' said Alessandra, and she grasped the bicycle firmly, wheeled it along the path and rested it against the wall of the house.

Now that she was in the tiny garden Saskia could see how the house was entered at two levels. The ground floor and the first floor must be connected within by a staircase. And the second level, the attic, had its own outside door. Saskia raised her head to look at it.

And as she did something chimed in her head.

I know this place.

There was a path here that led to the stairs beyond the kitchen window and there were twenty steep steps to climb to the door that led into the second floor. She knew that as certainly as she knew anything.

Twenty steps. Hewn out of the rock.

But how did she know this?

Her driver, Neil Buchan, was speaking to her aunt.

'She's a Granton all right. I'd've kent her in any crowd. She's your living image at that age. As like you as life.'

'She's like herself,' Saskia's great-aunt said sharply.

Neil dropped his eyes, then raised them again, looking into Alessandra's face.

'Let me pay you now, Neil Buchan.' Alessandra thrust some paper money into the taxi driver's hand.

Neil's face went red. 'Och, Alessandra, dinna worry aboot that the noo.'

But Alessandra forced him to accept the money, and he went away still muttering a protest. Alessandra took Saskia by the arm. 'Come inside,' she said. 'Come inside.'

As Saskia followed Alessandra indoors she imagined that within the impassiveness of her great-aunt's face there was a small smile of victory.

However, once inside the house Alessandra stopped, and she too looked intently at Saskia's face. Taking Saskia's chin firmly in her own fingers she turned her head this way and that, studying her features, her eyes coming to rest finally on her hair. It was the same colour as her own.

And Saskia saw it was also the same colour as Saskia's own father's hair. Burnt cinnamon, Saskia's mother called it, and when Saskia was small she had mixed the colour especially on her artist's palette for Saskia. But where Saskia's hair had flashes of red and copper Alessandra's hair showed grey.

'There's no denying where you come from,' Alessandra said at last and she sighed, a long exhalation of breath that contained resignation. 'But what you make of it is for you to decide.' She turned away then and went towards the kitchen and, as Saskia hesitated, she called over her shoulder, 'Come. Come. You must be starving. There's food here.'

There was food, plenty of it: soup, potatoes, stew, fish pie, vegetable quiche, trifle, cake, ice cream.

'I didn't know what you'd like to eat.' Alessandra waved her hand nervously over the selection of dishes on the kitchen worktop. 'It's been so long since I had any visitors. I know a lot of young people are vegetarian. Are you?'

'For preference, yes,' said Saskia, 'but don't go to any trouble, Great-aunt Alessandra. I can see to myself.'

'Saskia, please just call me by my name.' Alessandra gave a wry smile. 'I know that I am sister to your grand-father, but I don't feel particularly qualified to be anybody's great-aunt.' Alessandra paused and then continued, 'If you want to freshen up and telephone your parents to let them know that you have arrived safely, I'll warm some of these for you.'

Using the phone in the hall Saskia called home and sighed as the answering machine came on. 'It's me,' she paused, and then added, 'Saskia . . .' She waited, but no one at the other end rushed to pick up the receiver. She'd better be quick with her message. By the number of clicks she knew that there wasn't much space on the tape. It would be filled with her parents' friends and acquain-tances calling to make dates: Rotary Club dinners, golf club fixtures, the Ladies' Art Group classes, beauty salon appointments, luncheon club outings. Saskia spoke briefly.

As she returned to the kitchen her aunt asked her, 'Was Neil Buchan on time to collect you from the station?'

'Oh yes,' said Saskia. She felt obliged to defend her driver, who had tried to be kind to her in his own quiet way. 'He stopped on the road to point out the house. The setting is magnificent and so unusual, hewn out of the rock, with those outside steps leading to the second floor.'

There was a silence for about half a minute and then Alessandra said, 'I don't use the attic at all now. I've a bit of arthritis and it stops me going up and down stairs a lot. And ever since the roof was damaged I'm not sure how safe the floor is. Probably best to stay out of the attic at the moment, although I know that you used to like to play there.'

Saskia eyes opened wide in surprise. 'I did?'

'You don't remember.' Her aunt's voice sounded sad.

Saskia shook her head. 'Not at all.' And then, hesitating, said, 'Yet something is familiar.'

'It was a long time ago. You came in the summer when you were small. We walked on the beach together every day.'

'How strange,' said Saskia. 'I don't remember that. Except . . . are there twenty outside steps to the top floor?'

'Why yes!' Alessandra's face seemed to show genuine delight. 'You used to count them carefully each time you went up there.'

'Really?' Saskia shook her head, puzzled. 'I wonder why I have no memory of being here?'

'Your parents told me that you took very ill the winter after your last visit here. It was when you were still quite young. Perhaps that made you forget.'

'Perhaps . . .' Saskia thought slowly. She remembered being ill: not the actual illness, but the fact that she had been very, very sick. There was whispering; the doctor, a nurse, nurses that came, and then . . . the arguing.

Her parents shouting at each other constantly, and the ceaseless bickering. As she grew older Saskia had pushed all memories of that time away, connecting their arguing with her illness – becoming convinced that her being sick had caused her parents so much stress that they had fallen out and never become friends again. She was more mature now, and knew that if parents argued it was not a child's fault. Almost half of her friends had parents who were divorced or had difficulties in their marriages, so she felt less personal guilt about it. Her brain, her intellect, told her that her parents' differences were their problem, but her senses tried to tell her something else. Locked in her head was a feeling that somehow she had soured her mother and father's love for each other. Logic said that her instinct lied, but it was this instinct that controlled her emotions and her responses. Even now Saskia's mind swerved away from considering the subject. She looked up at her great-aunt.

'Truly I don't remember, but now that I'm here it may come back to me.'

Alessandra's face had returned to its former look of reserve. She inclined her head a little. 'We'll talk more in the morning. Now, I think you should rest.'

Saskia was so exhausted she barely had the energy to change into her nightclothes. As she fell upon the bed her last waking thought was, why *did* she have no memories of her time spent in this particular house?

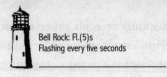

Chapter 3

That night Saskia did remember.

And as Saskia remembered, she dreamed. Of strange sights and sounds, and of the days on the beach below the house. Gathering seashells and other treasures along the shoreline, bringing them into her great-aunt's house, sorting out her collections, washing and polishing her 'gemstones'.

Familiar now are those sensations. Sand between her fingers and under her feet, bare feet in open sandals. She looks down at her ten baby toes with their pink half-moon nails curled in her little leather sandals. Squirming and pressing down with her heels makes dry sand wedge up between her toes and spill over her feet. The warm gritty granules run out as she walks on towards the water. Smooth driftwood sculpted by the sea is in her hands. Striated stone by the breakwater scrapes her fingers as she pulls away periwinkles and drops them into her bucket. There are heaps of shells at the far end of the beach, cockles and clams and mussels piled near some huge rocks. They are cool, these pale shells resting in the shadow of the cliff overhang. She is choosy and selects with care, one for its colour, another for its shape,

smooth or ridged for difference: her collection will have diversity.
At the foot of the tallest rock she finds a real treasure — it is a
giant whelk, Alessandra tells her, with a great ascending spiral,
and below this, a long fluted opening running down one side.
Saskia grasps it tightly. It is almost four times the size of her
hand, her small fingers cannot curl completely around it, but she
holds it pressed into her soft palm. Then she brings it close to her
face to study the single caramel-coloured conical whorl, the ever-
diminishing circular stairway leading to a dizzyingly minute
point. This shape, beyond her defining, beyond her imagining,
intoxicates her with its intricacies and its secret places. Who lives
within? Just around the curve where she cannot see? In her mind
she creates a miniature world inhabited by an infinite variety of
beings, all at her command. She breathes on the pink shadowed
entrance. Today she will be a kindly giant, her breath soft and
warm so as not to disturb the tiny inhabitants.

Then Alessandra stands in Saskia's dream. Between the child
Saskia and the shadowed rocks. Alessandra holds out her hand.
'The sea is more magical than you or I can believe. There are
places in the deep which will always be unknown.'

Salt water is on Saskia's face, she can taste it on her tongue,
but it is not sea spray.

Why is she crying?

It had been the year of the great gales. There had been a
storm. A violent reckless storm of no purpose. In the
morning they had watched the cauldron sea from
the front windows, and then, in the afternoon, had stood
in the lee of the sheltering wall of the house. Out on the
horizon the clouds had banked high with thunderous
rain and the wind had tossed the sea birds and driven

them against the cliffs. The rain had come, lancing horizontal, stinging face and hands. Saskia's mother, headscarf tightly knotted under her chin, had moaned about the downpour. Her father had quickly become bored. Both parents had complained of the wet and cold and gone indoors. Saskia had pleaded to stay outside, and Alessandra had gathered Saskia inside her own great Inverness cape and together they had ventured up onto the road. Leaning into the wind they had walked to where they could see the rooftops of Fhindhaven. Great pounding waves thundered up through the wynds between the old fisher cottages. Below them water had slapped so high and with such force against the rock face that it turned over on itself before crashing back down into the sea. Saskia, screaming in fear and excitement, had buried her face in her great-aunt's skirt. Alessandra had held her tightly.

'Nae to be frichtened, little quine. Alessandra's here. Nae to be frichtened.'

That night part of the roof of her great-aunt's house had blown away, the wind ripping slates off like cascading dominoes, smashing them against the rocks, hurling them into the ocean below.

In front of her now Saskia saw the scene the morning after the storm:

Herself, excited at having been close to danger and triumphant that she had emerged unscathed, charging about the garden among the debris. Smashed tiles, broken plant pots, uprooted bushes were strewn in chaos. Her father had cut his wrist trying to clear up, and now, disturbed and angry, was shouting down at Alessandra from the rooftop where he was attempting to nail back the torn felt.

'I told you last time we were here to get this roof seen to!'

Her great-aunt, quiet in the face of his fury, hands clasped together in front of her, said nothing.

Her mother, glancing anxiously from one to the other, watched Alessandra deal with her husband's rage.

Saskia's father descended the ladder, holding his wrist where he had ripped the skin, flung the old piece of felt from him, and yelled, 'You will have to fix this now, woman!'

Alessandra waited a moment, said three words. 'I will not.'

Later Saskia heard her father say to her mother, 'Alessandra is your typical perverse female. As soon as I told her that the house roof needed fixing she determined that she wouldn't do it.'

'You didn't tell her that it needed fixing.' Saskia's mother spoke carefully. 'You told her to fix it.'

'What's the difference?'

'All the difference in the world.'

They had never again been invited to spend holidays at Cliff House.

The sea also remembers . . .

Confirming the spring equinox the sun ascends into the sign of Aries and the coastal waters warm to receive the new hatching. The herring come through the Minch, and on, flowing past the Orkney and Shetland Islands. In many thousands cod begin to gather, lying in

17

by the coast of North America and Iceland. Halibut and sole congregate off south Greenland, haddock and plaice by the heel of Norway. From the rim of the Arctic Circle, extending in a vast widening sweep, the waters of the sea breathe new life, and in the depths of the oceans the paths of ancient glacial rivers ribbon out, pulling their migrants home.

Chapter 4

Something had happened.

Saskia rolled over in bed and struggled out of her dream. A slurring sound on the floorboards above and then a flittering noise. Caught between falling asleep again and awakening, she again heard the soft movement almost directly above her head.

Unsure of the location of the bedside lamp, Saskia reached for her torch in the rucksack lying beside the bed and sat up, more curious than frightened. The beam of the torch showed pale amber. Saskia shook it in irritation; she had forgotten to buy batteries. The light wavered, but casting around her showed that there was nothing in the bedroom except herself. Her great-aunt had told her that the house was never still. Window frames rattled, floorboards creaked, and there were any amount of other sounds caused by the proximity of the cliff and how it integrated with the structure of the house. Was the noise she heard of human origin? The only other person in the house was Alessandra, but her great-aunt had said that she did not go up to the second floor, and Saskia had seen her enter her room

19

on the ground floor when they had both gone to bed.

Saskia waited. The soft noise came again like a foot-fall in snow.

These were not normal night-time sounds, Saskia decided, nor the random groaning of an old house. And quickly, before the thought had a chance to grow, she rejected the idea of a ghost. It was more like an animal of some sort. She shivered: hopefully not rats. Saskia listened. Outside was the shush of the water, and then, more quietly than before, the flittering sound. It definitely came from the floor above. Saskia got up, and in doing so banged her knee on the edge of the bed and let out a cry, and then knew for sure that what had made the noise was of this world because it stopped immediately. Again Saskia waited. In the house was utter silence.

Saskia's first few months of her gap year backpacking in Nepal had accustomed her to being in the dark, or in unusual places. Silences did not intimidate her and her scientific brain refused to accommodate the super-natural. It was a bird, she decided, one of the many sea birds she had seen on the drive north. Spring was approaching, they'd be building nests on the cliff, one of them must be in the upper room. The whole back wall of the house was embedded into and supported by the cliff, and her bedroom was situated at the rear of the house. She could probably see the nest from her window. With the dim glow of her torch to show her the way she crossed the room and lifted aside the curtain just a little. The cliff face loomed close, etched black and dark grey by a pale moon. Saskia looked down. The tide was in.

A strange flickering light reflected from the water below her.

Quietly Saskia clicked off her torch and walked forward. She let the curtain fall behind her so that she stood in the dark space between it and the window. The light on the water undulated as the waves moved. Saskia raised her eyes to look out to sea. The moon was shadowed but towards the horizon the sky in the northern hemisphere glowed. She knew that during summer so far north the sky never got properly dark, that the sun's orbit circled low, skirting the earth's perimeter throughout the night. But it was too early in the year for that. And this light that she could see was not constant, such as dawn light might be. It pulsated with a restlessness that did not seem in keeping with anything man-made.

Saskia took another step closer to the window glass, when suddenly, spanning the whole arc of her vision, a rippling cascading sheet of burnished colours appeared silently across the dark sky. What rising planet could trail such streams of rainbowed vapour? It came to Saskia slowly that what she was seeing must be the aurora borealis. Merging, dividing, re-merging, a veil of incandescent colour trembled in the heavens, while, with languid graceful energy, shimmering lucent violets and yellows and mauves flowed through the sky, twisting among the stars.

Entranced, Saskia kneeled down on the floor under the window and gazed at the great chromatic columns, forming and re-forming, dissolving shifting draperies of light. She watched until she grew quite cold, and dawn

came around four a.m. And as she watched she forgot
everything else: her strange dreams during the earlier
part of the night, her fears and unhappiness at home, her
vague uneasiness about her memories of this house.

Chapter 5

Forgot, that is, until the next morning when she joined her great-aunt in the kitchen and mentioned that she had seen the aurora borealis.

'Aaah . . .' said Alessandra. 'The northern lights.' She paused in setting out breakfast things. 'They are very beautiful.' She opened a cupboard and took down boxes of cereal. 'They're sometimes called the "Heavenly Dancers", and when you watch how they move, you understand why. It's years since I saw them.'

Saskia seized the moment. 'So you weren't up and about last night?'

Upon Alessandra's face came a quick shaded look. 'Why do you ask?'

'There was a noise . . . well, I thought I heard a noise . . . In the attic.'

'I may have visited the toilet,' said Alessandra awkwardly. 'Sometimes I go in the night, but I don't always remember if I did or not.' She laid breakfast dishes on the kitchen table with careful movements, two brown bowls, two spoons, two mugs.

There was silence in the kitchen. Saskia looked up.

23

Alessandra had stopped in the middle of her task. Her hands hovered. She saw that Saskia had noticed and quickly she clasped them together. After a moment she smiled at Saskia. 'A bird may be trapped inside the roof. I'm afraid that I've not kept the house in as good repair as I should have. I'll go up to the top floor and . . . make sure that it is secure. Then you can go and explore. You probably want to see if any of your things are still there?'

'My things?'

'It's where you used to keep your treasures,' said Alessandra. She poured tea for both of them and then sat down opposite Saskia.

Her 'treasures'. Saskia's mind lingered on the word. It had been in her head recently. In a dream. Last night in her dream. When she was small she had collected things on the beach. She had called them her treasures.

'Last night I had a dream about us,' said Saskia, 'you and me, being on the beach together. I was quite young and we were picking up things and putting them in my bucket.'

'Yes, we did that many times. You had a great hoard of objects that you collected.'

'How often did I visit this house?'

'Every year, from when you were a toddler until you were about six or seven.'

'Why don't I remember anything at all?' asked Saskia.

'I don't know,' said Alessandra. Her eyes met Saskia's and slid away. 'There is no reason I can think of. Perhaps your dream of last night is you beginning to recall your childhood memories.'

'It was so specific,' said Saskia. 'I could hear the gulls, smell the sea. And then, in another part of my dream, there was a great gale and you and I were watching the sea on the clifftop above the village. I was terribly pleased because my parents had gone back into the house and I thought I was very brave.'

For an instant Saskia saw something come alive in her great-aunt's eyes.

'I too recall that day very well,' said Alessandra.

'You spoke in a different language,' said Saskia, 'telling me not to be scared. You called me a strange name, it sounded like "kwine".'

'*Quine*,' said her great-aunt. 'It's Doric, the language of the Northeast. "Quine" is like "queen", but here it means girl, little girl, young woman. It was a tremendous hurricane as I recall, out of season, unexpected, and I was excited so I would lapse into the language of my youth. I don't speak it now . . . at least very little.'

Saskia frowned and reeled back in her mind the images from last night's dream. 'For some reason my father was very angry with you on the morning after the gale. Part of the roof had blown off and he was shouting at you.'

'Yes, he *was* very annoyed about the state of the roof,' said Alessandra. 'He always did get angry when people did not do as he wished.'

'Why did I not remember such an exciting event before now?'

'There are reasons why we forget or choose to forget,' said Alessandra. 'Your memories of this house will come back to you in time.'

'You can't "choose" to forget,' said Saskia. 'By definition, that is impossible.'

'I'd forgotten how logically the young argue.' Alessandra spoke carefully. 'I suppose what I mean is that your mind has the ability to block out certain things. There are different reasons why people forget. It may be tied with another more unpleasant circumstance, or linked to something that you are avoiding dealing with.'

'Like you avoided dealing with the roof?' Saskia put her hand to her mouth. The words had come out before she realized how rude they sounded. 'I'm sorry,' she said. 'I didn't mean to be so rude.'

There was a tiny pause, then Alessandra gave a brief smile. 'I don't think you rude, Saskia. Perhaps I was "being perverse". That's what your father told me at the time. He said I was being perverse.'

'Were you?'

'No . . . Well yes, I suppose I was. I just didn't like his manner. I've had to live a hard frugal life to keep this house, and I resented his way of advising me.'

'I see it now,' Saskia spoke slowly. 'He was ordering you about. But then, he says that you do need to be told what to do, especially now that you are—' Saskia floundered in embarrassment.

Alessandra raised her eyebrows. 'Ah, senility. Is that what they say about me now?'

Saskia looked at her great-aunt. Her eyes showed no cloudiness, none of the vague abstraction with which some old people looked out at the world. Again she thought of Alessandra's age. Her great-aunt had been a teenager when Saskia's father was born – in fact, the age I am now, Saskia suddenly realized.

'In my dream,' said Saskia, 'you led me away from the rocks . . .'

Alessandra eyes recoiled from Saskia's look. 'What rocks?' She stirred her tea with unnecessary attention.

'The rocks at the far end of the beach.'

'Did I?'

'Yes.' Saskia studied her great-aunt's face. It showed no emotion, but the hand that held the teaspoon trembled.

'That end of the beach is not a safe place,' said Alessandra. 'There are constant rock falls from the cliff, especially in bad weather.'

'You said the sea was magical.'

'That's what you dreamed I said.' Alessandra smiled, it seemed to Saskia, with difficulty. 'It is much more likely that what I said was, "Those rocks are dangerous." They were dangerous then. They are dangerous now.'

When, Saskia wondered, did *magical* become *dangerous*?

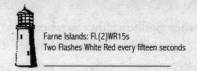
Chapter 6

After breakfast Alessandra showed Saskia around the house.

On the first floor, across the landing from the bath-room and Saskia's bedroom, were two more bedrooms looking out to the east with views over the little beach below the house.

'My brother, who was your grandfather, had one of these rooms and I the other.' Alessandra paused and smiled as if a small secret memory had passed through her mind. 'Rob was the best brother I could wish for. He was a very loving and good person. And Esther, his wife, was as sweet and kind as he was. They were well matched.' She sighed. 'I loved them both dearly.'

'You must have been sad when he moved away to get married.'

'To begin with they lived here. Even after my brother was killed at sea, Esther stayed on. Your father was born in this house.' Alessandra moved to the window and spoke with her back to Saskia. 'It was later on . . . your father was still very young, not much more than a baby, when your grandmother Esther took him to

28

Yarmouth to be with her own people.'

The rooms were sparsely furnished and bare of decoration, with no prints or photographs on display, and when Saskia asked about family photographs her great-aunt said, 'My father did not like photographs being taken, but I have my own photograph albums that you can look through.'

Downstairs, on the ground floor, running along the back of the house was another bathroom and the kitchen. To the front were Alessandra's bedroom and a long drawing/dining room with tall windows facing east. A pelmet of burgundy velour framed the windows but no curtains hung on either side. A pair of binoculars rested on the window ledge.

'What a stunning view!' said Saskia. 'No wonder you don't have curtains. I wouldn't even close the window blinds if I lived in this house.'

'I never do . . . now,' said Alessandra.

The huge old dining table was covered with papers, books, magazines, journals and photographs. Beside an old typewriter stood a portable tape recorder.

'It looks a bit of a muddle but when I'm working I do know where everything is.'

Saskia blushed, thinking her aunt was referring to her earlier remark about dementia. 'Working?' she asked quickly to cover her embarrassment.

'I'm collating personal local histories. It's mainly labelling photographs and doing one or two taped inter-views for our new Heritage Centre. Sometimes, if the weather is kind and I'm feeling up to it, I cycle out and take photographs of the little towns and the bays. It's all changing so rapidly. When Rob and I were growing up you could walk across the boats from one end of Fhindhaven harbour to the other. Now the harbour has more pleasure craft than working boats. With the oil boom going on and us merging with Europe everything is changing. A lot of our heritage will soon be gone for ever.'

Alessandra leaned over and pressed the PLAY button on the tape recorder. 'My hearing is not what it was,' she said and turned the sound up.

The voice of an old man filled the room.

'Ye want me to tell ye whit it was tae be a fisherman?' The man laughed. 'The hale thing, like? Sixty-twa years in five meenits?'

'Jist little things, Dodie. Wee bit memories . . . ken?' Saskia barely recognized her great-aunt's voice on the tape.

'Dinna ken whaur tae begin, Alessandra.'

Alessandra's voice spoke again: gentle, encouraging. 'My brother Rob a'ways said the herring drifters were the real fishing boats.'

'Aye, well, thon were the days afore the war when ye followed the herring through the seasons as they moved roon the mainland. The "magic circle" we ca'd it, but noo the scientists tell us different. From the Western Isles up bye Shetland and then aff Peterheid tae the far banks and doon the coast to the English gruns, then roon and up by Ireland they went.'

Saskia moved closer trying to tune her ear to pick up the unfamiliar accent.

'An' it was oor job tae find them. It was hard work and

ye needed tae ken the ways o' the fish. Ye never kent if it would be a big catch or nae, but that's whit gave the herring fishing an edge ower line fishing and attracted a lot o' the young ones tae it. There's an excitement on the boat as ye leave and sail awa' . . . sail awa' to the high seas and deep watter.'

'Tell us then aboot bein' at sea,' Alessandra urged him gently.

'It was a hunt, ken? Ye'd tae set yer course and ken the signs that would tell ye whaur the fish micht be. Ye'd look oot for dolphins or birds diving. Noo they've got modern methods. But where's the interest in watching for a bleep on a screen? A guid skipper could feel his way to the herring gruns blindfold, he'd smell the herring, see the plankton glistening upon the watter.'

'Rob, my brother, said they'd sometimes use landmarks to guide them oot,' said Alessandra.

'Oh, aye,' the old fisherman went on. 'As ye left ye'd line the boat up wi' the high steeple in the Broch or the lighthouse on Kinnaird Point, and ye'd guess how many miles oot the shoals were. And when ye got tae the fishing gruns, once ye'd found yer mark, the skipper would put the boat afore the wind, and then ye'd shoot the nets. Doon and doon they'd fall, like a great lang curtain in the sea. Then he'd bring the boat roon, head tae wind, and let her drift with the tide. And ye're hopin' yer skipper's nose is keen an' his een sharp an' ye are on top o' the shoals. The herring a' move together and try tae swim through the nets and get caught by the gills. An ye bide that way for a few hours or more, an if the weather turns heavy ye let oot more rope if needed tae keep the boat right balanced. An' after a bit we draw in oor harvest. We'd shout tae be heard above the wind and the noise, and the birds screaming and plunging intae the fish. We'd begin to drag the nets up and ower the side. The winch taks up the messenger rope but the men hauled the nets, an' they were heavy, fu' o' fish.'

'Did ye sing, at all?'

'Sing? Nae. Not so often. But we'd call tae each other as we hauled the nets, an' try to get a motion tae it. Haul and shake, haul and shake. Backbreaking, aye, back-breaking. With the force o' the waves against ye, rain streamin' doon yer oilskins and the boat battling the sea: tossing, riding high, an' then troughing doon and doon until ye thocht it wasnae gan tae cam' back up, and ye trying tae keep yer feet as ye pulled for dear life.

'Aye . . . Mind, there *was* one song . . .' Suddenly the old fisherman began to sing.

> *'Haul away, boys!*
> *Haul away, me lads.*
> *Fill the boat, me boys!*
> *Wi' the bonnie siller herring . . .'*

There was a silence. Then after a moment the fisherman began to speak again. 'Ye see, when the nets are a' adrift and ye can feel the drag, it tells ye the shoals are there, thoosans of fish sweemin' awa' under the boat, then ye ken fine the sicht yer gan tae see when ye begin the haul up. And the anticipation o' it is in yer belly, an yer eyes are na'whaur else but on the watter. There's naethin' quite like it and Ah canna right describe it tae ye. There's

32

the surge in yer heart when ye ken the nets is fu' and yer gaun home tae harbour wi' a full catch. An' the mate shouts an' the winch creaks, an' the first net breaks up through the waves, an' there across the face o' the deep are the fish, thrashing an' twisting, an' glittering silver – as if the lady moon hersel' had tumbled fae the night sky and splintered intae a million siller pieces scattered ower the surface of the sea.

'And we'd pull then, pull hard, for hours, hand over hand, bringin' them in. And as they cam' up we cried oot, "*Swim up! Swim up! Ye siller darlin's!*" '

The tape whirred and ran on, clicking to a stop at the end.

Saskia broke the silence first. 'That was beautiful,' she said. 'He has the sound of the sea in his voice.'

Two spots of pleasure glowed in Alessandra's cheeks. 'I thought so too,' she said. 'Although it loses a little when transcribed to the page. It is a language with its own music.'

'I didn't catch all of it,' said Saskia, 'but it doesn't seem to matter somehow.' She wandered over to the row of glass-fronted bookcases. 'You called him "Dodie". Is that a local name?'

'It's for George. But here in the Northeast we have lots of by-names.'

'By-name?' Saskia interrupted. 'Do you mean like a nickname?'

'Yes,' said Alessandra. 'They are used widely here because there are so many common surnames and first names. In small villages, if everyone was called a name like Smith, and children were always named for parents and grandparents, then a village could have a dozen or so people with exactly the same first and last names. So people are individualized by attaching a by-name like Pendy or Curly or Bullan, or some such thing. Sometimes they use the mother or father's name first. Just as in the Western Isles MacDonald originally meant child of Donald, here in the Northeast we might say Annie's Dodie. And a son of Dodie also called Dodie could be known as Dodie's Dodie.'

'Dodie's Dodie?' Saskia laughed.

Alessandra smiled. 'Yes, even to the extent that we do have a man who is called Dodie's Dodie's Dodie.'

'What would I be?' asked Saskia.

'You?' said Alessandra. Her gaze shifted and she looked beyond Saskia's head and out to sea. 'You are Saskia.'

'But,' Saskia persisted, 'if my grandfather's name was Rob, and my father's name is Alexander, then my father is not named for his father. Is my father named for his own grandfather?'

Alessandra blinked and refocused her eyes on Saskia. 'Your father? Named for *my* father? No. Not for him.'

'Who then?'

'For me.' Alessandra spoke quietly. 'Your grandmother named her baby for me.'

Saskia turned to the glass-fronted bookcase to look at the photograph albums, and as she did so she saw the expression on her aunt's face. Not pride, as one might expect at having a child named for her. Not pride, no. Alessandra's face in the glass was crowded with grief. But when Saskia turned to look directly at

34

her great-aunt the crumpled look of sorrow was gone.

'You asked about photographs when we were upstairs.' Alessandra reached past Saskia, opened one of the bookcase doors and took out some old-fashioned photograph albums. 'Here are all the family albums: your Granton ancestors. Not so many from when Rob and I were young. My father would not agree to such things, so it was only on rare occasions that we had a photograph taken. But your grandparents' wedding photograph is there, and . . . your own family holiday album.' She held out a thick book to Saskia and stood back looking at her as she opened it up.

She must think that this will make me remember my previous visits here, thought Saskia. 'Did I look through these when I was younger?' she asked Alessandra. 'You would think I would remember doing that.'

'They didn't interest you very much,' said her great-aunt. 'You were more inclined to be outside playing. We could hardly keep you indoors.'

The album was set out in years, the photographs attached to the dark-brown pages with old-fashioned corner mounts and labelled in careful small script: '*Saskia holding a crab*', '*Saskia at the harbour*', '*Saskia with an ice-cream cone*', '*Saskia with her mum and dad*'. Saskia looked more closely at this photograph of a happy family. *Had* they been happy then? Both her parents were smiling into the camera, but then they were good at putting on a show for the sake of appearances. Saskia became aware that Alessandra was watching her face. She leafed through the last few pages and saw a photograph of a little girl squinting at the camera holding something in her hand.

'It's the shell!' cried Saskia. 'I dreamed about it last night. The special great whelk. I loved my shell collection, and that one in particular.'

Saskia's mind jolted. A real memory slotted into place, not a recollection of her dream of last night.

She is sitting at the kitchen table, her legs swinging free, banging her sandals against the chair.

'I want to go out. I want to go out. Out. Out. Out,' she chants.

Her great-aunt Alessandra turns from the stove, smiling.

'We will go out, my love,' she sings back. 'We will go out together. Out. Out. Out.'

Saskia looked at her great-aunt. 'We *did* walk on the beach every day. I remember now, gulping down my food quickly so that we could go outside. The days seemed long and warm and . . . and . . . happy.'

Alessandra nodded. 'The last year ye visited me was an especially grand summer, until the night of the storm.' She took the book from Saskia's hand, closed it softly and replaced it in the bookcase.

'Why did we not come back?' Saskia asked.

'Maybe you just grew out of it.' Alessandra's voice was light but the line of her lip was pressed thin. 'Your father said that you wanted to go to Disneyland, and at that time his business began to expand. As he was making so much money he could afford to take you there.'

Saskia knew that she had been much more interested in Sea World than Disneyland. The dolphins and whales had attracted her greatly, the great sea beasts that had known the ways of the planet long before man had evolved. Another thought came to Saskia. Was that when she had started trying to please her father? Becoming anxious to do what she thought would win his favour rather than doing what she herself wanted to do; feigning interest in exhibits and topics that interested him? But then, didn't all little girls do the same thing at that age? Saskia had gone on to develop a close relationship with her father. She found that they shared the same sense of humour, enjoyed similar kinds of food, and relished outdoor activities, unlike her mother, whose preferred hobbies were reading or gardening or painting.

'I wasn't really surprised when your father said that you were so keen to visit here again now,' Alessandra went on, 'but I didn't realize that you would have so few childhood memories of this place. Come, I'll show you outside.'

Saskia was glad Alessandra was walking ahead of her so that she did not catch her reaction. Saskia knew that it was the other way about. Her father had told her that it was Alessandra who had written and invited Saskia to visit her. Perhaps her great-aunt was too proud to admit that.

The outside walls of the house which faced the sea had a thin gravel path running round them. Saskia walked all the way to the end of this path past the ground-floor windows at the front, to the side where her bedroom overlooked the sea. Here the path dribbled out to finish up against the cliff. On the outside edge of the path was a thick stone wall, and beyond that the cliff fell away sharply.

'Wow!' said Saskia. 'It must have taken some amount of work to build a house in this place.'

'It was my mother's father who built it. I don't remember him at all. He died before I was born. He came from Buckie and the folk of Buckie have the reputation of being the hardiest in the Northeast. They say my grandfather loved the sea and this house made him feel as if he was part of it.'

'When it's very windy do you ever feel the house might blow away?'

Alessandra shook her head. 'Never. It is solid within the rock. The back wall is buried into the overhang, secure, like an eagle's nest.'

They returned to the little garden where, at the start of the front wall, the stairs led down to the beach. This gable end of the house, which faced inland, was where both entrances to the house were, the main door leading to the hall and to the left of that the kitchen door. Alessandra showed Saskia her vegetable and herb garden.

'It doesn't look much but it's very sheltered and gives a good crop.' She stopped by the stairs that led to the top floor of the house. 'I put your bicycle with my own in this little cellar beside the kitchen door. Because it is under these outside stairs that go up to the attic it runs a little way back into the rock.'

The cellar door was unlocked and as Saskia followed Alessandra inside she saw that it was really a room cut out of the cliff. The sides and back wall were rock, part of the cliff itself.

'Some houses along the coast had rooms like this or

caves behind them. They say that they were used in the last century for smuggled goods. I keep only my bicycle in there now.'

Her aunt stood at the door as Saskia went in to explore. It was much darker at the far end where the sunlight did not reach.

'There's nothing much further back there. There were always rumours that a passageway led into the cliffs with a secret path to Fhindhaven or the top road. Locals made up stories of treasure and buried pirate's gold. When we were small Neil Buchan and I searched for it but it doesn't exist.'

Rumours of treasure. Saskia smiled to herself. Her father must have absorbed these stories and now he fancied that there was money hidden in the house. In reality everything about her great-aunt and the house gave the appearance of lack of wealth. The plainness of Alessandra's clothes (she had on today the same clothes she had worn yesterday), the bareness of the rooms, the worn parts on the treads of the stair carpet. There was nothing of any great value in the cellar: an axe for chopping firewood, a small boat anchor, herring barrels of different sizes, and a whaling harpoon, its tip marked with rust.

'You could probably sell this stuff to a museum,' said Saskia. She walked forward and touched one of the old herring barrels where a crown and some letters had been branded onto the wood. 'What do the different symbols mean?'

'It tells you what's in them. The fish were graded, and the crown stamp means that it's certified.' Alessandra hesitated in the doorway. 'I packed herring for a few years when I was a young girl, that's how I know.'

They went out, and Alessandra pulled the door over behind them.

Chapter 7

In the late morning Saskia walked on the beach.

Looking towards the land from the shore she could appreciate the setting of the house, and how neatly it sat in its niche in the cliff. She couldn't see her own bedroom window. It was on the same side of the house as the downstairs bathroom. Both faced north, away from the beach and the road. Saskia's eyes looked along the tiny windows of the attic. She could see busy movement around the upper part of the house as birds sought suitable nesting spots on the cliff face.

Saskia sat down on the shingle that ran in a narrow strand under the cliff. She took off her trainers and socks, placed them beside her and, with arms wrapped around her knees, gazed at the sea for a time. She did not care that it was not a holiday-brochure type beach or a sultry summer's day. The sky was overcast and the water restless, its surface stippled white and grey, yet clear light came from the distant horizon and settled in her.

Saskia screwed up her eyes and saw a trawler or two pass by out at sea and then the flat outline of a tanker. This morning Alessandra had told Saskia that she and

41

her brother, Saskia's grandfather, had stood together on the beach steps as children and watched the fishing fleet leave Fhindhaven at the start of the season – such a crush of boats that there was little space to see daylight between them. That had been in the days of the herring drifters. Now the boats used different methods and fished for white fish: cod, haddock and whiting. 'The two world wars ended the main herring markets for us,' said Alessandra, 'and in more recent years the herring stocks failed. It was an industry which originally owed much to poverty and slavery. In the past herring was used as cheap food to feed Eastern Europe and the slaves in the Americas. We fed the world with herring but now our fishermen have to search for a different harvest.'

Within the vastness of the ocean, Saskia knew, there were more species of marine life than ever had been, or would be, upon the land – more than the birds, amphibians, reptiles and all the mammals put together. When she was younger she had been a fact collector. One of those children (she smiled now to think of her former irritating self) who absorbed information like a sponge and squirted it back out at any opportunity, pestering grown-ups with her knowledge.

'Do you know that there are over one million, million herring? That's more than five times the human population on the planet.'

'Who counted them?' her father asks.

'Do you know that some fish can actually talk to each other?'

'Wouldn't it be nice if you stopped talking occasionally?' her mother says pointedly.

'Do you know that a salmon can swim in the sea and in rivers?'

Her mother sighs.

'Do you know that parts of the ocean are deeper than Mount Everest is tall?'

'Miss "Do-you-know?",' her father teases her. 'Do you know it's rude to show off?'

The slight feeling of hurt stayed with her even now.

But then, she had grown into the age where she began to regard her parents critically. She'd evolved a manner of boorishness to annoy them, gradually behaving more and more ungraciously whenever an occasion presented itself. But it hadn't been a one-way dialogue of bad manners. Her mother was a master of the verbal put-down, smoothly despatching accurate barbs whose venom remained in the flesh long after the initial wounding; her father threatened uncontrolled rage, which was always to be avoided. Yet Saskia couldn't really blame either of them for reacting badly to her own tantrums, screaming fits, three-day sulks, or absolute rudeness to their friends and guests. But, as she fully entered her teenage years and stretched out to fingertip-reach the extremities of behaviour, she became aware that she could hold the balance of their peace in her hands. Instead of uniting together to sustain themselves against her wilful conduct, they began to use it, and her, to score points off each other in their own continuous war of attrition. Their remarks interchangeable between them.

★ ★ ★

43

'She never learned that language from me.'

'If you spent more time with your daughter then you'd be able to have a proper dialogue with her.'

'Another instance of bad temper/selfishness (fill in any transgression) that I have to put up with from the other occupants of this household.'

'I think you'll find that's exactly how you react to not having your own way.'

Saskia had returned from school one day to find them sniping at each other. Her mother, catching sight of her before her father did, had immediately burst into tears. Saskia had reacted at once.

'Daddy, don't make Mummy cry!' And she had run and flung her arms around her mother's neck, and then caught the glance of triumph that her mother had given her father.

As she grew older she had resolved to try not to be part of it.

It had been made easier that several of her classmates had serious parent problems – or, more correctly, parents with problems, her friend Gideon had corrected her. Gideon's parents had not spoken directly to each other for eighteen months and communicated through him.

'Gideon, will you ask your father if he intends using the car this evening?'

'Gideon, please inform your mother that I will not be present at dinner tonight.'

Gideon was a natural clown and had entertained everyone in the sixth-form common room by relating the nightly 'Duels of the Dinner Table', as he called them.

'They say that they are staying together for the benefit of the children –' he had nodded gravely – 'and I have to agree. We are indeed benefiting. My young sister, who always longed to be slim, has lost about a stone and a half over the last year or so, and as for myself . . . well, I intend to become a playwright. When I'm supposed to be doing homework I am in fact writing down every stricken word that they make me say in lieu of speaking to each other. It will save me the effort of having to actually make up the dialogue for my own play. My first script should be ready for television quite soon. It will be a cutting-edge drama. Rather than *Room with a View* it will be more like *View with a Doom* – *a modern teenage perspective on cohabiting adults.* Desmond Morris can do an introduction. I think I'll call it *Naked Idiots.*' Everyone had laughed and Gideon had looked very pleased with himself.

But Saskia had seen him one morning getting out of his mother's car. Eyes filling up with tears, he brushed past her and went along the school corridor swearing, and kicking his rucksack viciously in front of him.

Her friend Persemone's parents shouted and threw things. Persemone had asked Saskia if she might keep some of her more precious possessions in Saskia's room for safekeeping. So Saskia fell heir to Persemone's collection of glass animals and a chocolate pot her Greek grandmother had given her as a christening present.

'These animals have more sense than our parents,' Persemone had confided in Saskia one evening, as she arranged and rearranged her ornaments on Saskia's windowsill.

And then, when her father finally admitted to the

affair he had long been accused of, Persemone had stormed round to Saskia's house and taken the animals and broken their legs deliberately; systematically snapping the fragile limbs one by one, moving on to the slender necks of her Bambi fawn and the elegant glass giraffe, executing them, not in temper, but in cold hatred. Finally lifting the chocolate pot with its Mediterranean colours, hot orange, cool blue and white, she had raised it above her head, casting about for a suitably hard surface to throw it down.

Saskia had leaped up and taken it from her friend's hand, replacing the lid and carefully setting it down on the windowsill. 'No, Mona. Don't destroy that. It came from your grandmother. A gift, to you, with love. It's not to do with your parents. Try not to be affected by their fights. You've got to resist the poison that spreads all around.'

'You have an antidote?' asked Persemone, beginning to cry.

'No,' said Saskia, and the two of them had wept together.

'We really do need to get a life,' snuffled Persemone. 'It's ridiculous that their moods affect us so badly.'

'We're in bondage,' said Saskia. 'Emotional slavery.'

Her mother had tutted when she had found out about the destruction in Saskia's room, and later said smugly, 'Continental blood, you see. Very little control over their emotions. Always have to go around screaming and smashing things.'

Sometimes Saskia believed that she might prefer that way of arguing, instead of the bottled-up resentment of her mother, who claimed that by putting her career as an artist on hold in the early years of her marriage, she had given up a promising future. Saskia's father openly scoffed at her, saying that no one had ever bought any of her paintings anyway, and that she enjoyed living a life of ease and not facing up to that fact. Her mother replied smartly that no doubt she had absorbed some of her partner's behaviour patterns over years of living with him, as he evaded any responsibility, especially if he could blame someone else. And they would have started yet another session of trading complaints had not Saskia interrupted to try to turn the conversation.

It came to Saskia then as she sat on the beach that perhaps this was a major factor in their deciding that she should attend university near home. She would be on hand as a buffer. Years earlier her father had advised her on subject choices for the university course he considered most suitable. At a parents' evening her career adviser at school had said, 'Why Saskia, I thought you'd choose something in the sciences. There is a whole range of courses in marine biology that might suit you.'

Her father had interrupted smoothly, 'I need my best girl doing accounts. It's already been decided.'

Her close relationship with her father survived the family squabbling. And he was so very, very good at getting his own way. He had bought her a pony that year as a reward for being mature and sensible. With the result that she felt mature and sensible, and had even offered to help him out with paperwork during her holidays. Although that had brought its own tensions. When she had tried to balance some columns of figures he had been evasive and finally had turned a cold look upon her and said, '*I* keep the order book. It is of no concern to anyone else.'

She had trembled before his anger and decided that she did not want to be on the receiving end of his rage. When her mother, overhearing, had enquired if there was anything the matter, Saskia had said, 'I don't understand how income is registered. I can follow the expenses; for the outgoings there's a clear paper trail. It's how the ingoings are credited that's a mystery to me.'

Her mother had replied, 'If you ever get your father to give a straight answer to a question do let me know. I'll mark it on the calendar.'

Her father had countered, 'If your mother was allowed to dabble in anything to do with the business it would be financial ruin for us all.'

Her one independent action had been her trip with her friends to Nepal after her last term at school. She had saved for it herself, using birthday and babysitting money, and her father had only found out about it when they had been deciding which part of the world to visit. By then it was too late for him to talk her out of changing her plans. She *was* going, she had promised herself. Once, just once, before she settled for study and then a life of account books and figures, she'd do something *she* wanted to. In the end he had become quite supportive. Buying geographical magazines, locating up-to-date maps of various countries, joining in the discussions as to what parts of the world were most interesting. On the night before she was due to leave he had even given her some extra spending money, and wished her 'bon voyage'.

'You have a great time.' He had ruffled her hair and nuzzled her ear. 'And I don't really mind you skiving off for a bit now that you've given your promise that when you return you'll do this degree in accounting and help me with the business.'

She had tried to protest, one last feeble attempt. 'Dad, you know I'm not sure that I'm the best person for your kind of work. I'm a bit woolly about the details involved in property development.'

'You have a very practical mind so don't worry about it. Anyway, who else would I leave the family fortune to? That's our deal. Off you go and enjoy yourself and when you come back I'll show you more of the ropes.'

It was only now she saw that, in effect, he'd told her what she was going to do with her life. That she was bound to a promise that she had not made.

Saskia rolled up the legs of her trousers and began to walk towards the sea. The thick soft yellow sand was warm between her toes. She stepped from the yellow to the paler cool sand, and then felt the firm hard wet sand under her feet, and saw the creamy purl of foam at the water's edge. The wind moved in her hair and she untied the scrunchie that secured it in place. The sun came out and she tilted her head back and shook her hair down about her shoulders. She kept facing seawards as she walked along the beach away from the house, and, because this little bay jutted out into the North Sea, her whole field of vision was the sea and the limitless possibility of the unknown. Had Christopher Columbus felt like this, alone on the ocean while his sailors slept, standing on the deck of his small ship? She had a sudden need to find out. She decided at that moment that one day she was going to sail round the world, one day . . .

She stopped.

She had quoted her mother.

'One day, I am going to. I am going to . . . going to. One day.'

Saskia gave her head a shake to rid herself of the thought. Was it inevitable? They said that you became like your parents whether you wanted to or not.

She bent to pick up an object on the shoreline. A little piece of green glass. It was as smooth as a pebble and must have come from a bottle many years ago. Saskia squinted through it at the light.

This is how a fish must view its world, she thought, blinking and looking around, with her eye still covered by the green glass. She remembered reading a description of the body of a fish, how some had a lateral line running along the centre of either side. A tube filled with fluid which reacted immediately to all sensations: heat and light and movement, changes in temperature and water pressure, registering the tiniest vibration in the waters surrounding it.

In the oceans of the world the shoals moved as one, responding to hidden signals, a sharp tug flipping the colours from vermilion and ochre to scarlet and yellow, from turquoise to jet. Colours more intense, more alive than anything her mother could conjure from tubes of paint.

Saskia imagined herself as a creature of the sea. Wind and waves streamed through her hair and she floated in the deep; legs, arms suspended, body buoyed up by the waters. With a twist, a quick flick of her mermaid's tail, she spiralled down and myriad tiny fish followed her. The colours shone on her skin.

Saskia walked on along the beach, drunk with the imagery, the assault on her senses, the vista of the sea and sky. And as she walked her feeling of exhilarating freedom merged with other similar ones from when she was very small, and she recognized them. But it was not just being part of the physical external landscape that she knew once again, her internal landscape too, was reawakenng with experiences that echoed the frequency of her own spirit.

She was now approaching the rocks at the far end. Dark, oddly shaped boulders, not, it seemed to her, fallen from above, but looking more as if piled up by some care-less giant in a clumsy attempt to build a wall. These were the rocks that her great-aunt had asked her to avoid. Black basalt, volcanic; residual leavings from the earth's groaning birth. The rocks at the near end of the beach close to the house were a less formidable barrier, curving gently round the northern headland to Fhindhaven. On this south side they plunged down into the sea, great jagged lumps of cliff, creating swift uncertain currents as the water rose and fell between them.

And as Saskia gazed at them, the solid outline changed and altered.

She stared. For a moment it seemed to her as if the rock itself had actually moved. Her eyes, adjusting from light to dark, took a second or two to focus. Saskia frowned and looked again. She was not mistaken. The rock *had* moved, or rather something on one of the rocks had moved and now lay still.

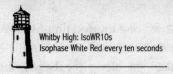

Chapter 8

The figure moved again, flopping from side to side as though in pain. Saskia squinted at the outline, grey against a grey sky.

'Do you need help?' she called out.

There was no reply. Saskia moved closer, and then she saw that it was a seal. A large grey seal. She was now near enough to hear that it was wheezing horribly. It lay with its head lolling, a rasping noise coming from its throat. Saskia stopped and then walked slowly towards the animal. Had it been caught in fishing lines, or wounded in some other way? She would have to climb onto the rocks a little bit if she wanted to see more clearly.

Saskia glanced guiltily at the house, and then tutted at herself in irritation. She felt that her great-aunt still regarded her as the small child she had played with many years ago, not the young adult she now was. Later Saskia would tell her how she had trekked through the high passes in the Nepalese hills, but for the moment she determined to climb up onto the nearest rock to have a look at the injured animal. As she did, the seal flopped over onto one side in alarm, and then tried to right itself, flippers waving hopelessly. It seemed to her to be very sick, every breath an effort, fluid dribbling from its mouth and nose, but she could see no obvious signs of injury. Saskia crouched down on the rock. Her being so close to the animal was making it agitated, and anyway, what could she do by staying beside it? There must be some sort of animal help organization nearby that she could contact. She decided she needed to return to her great-aunt's house and find out.

Saskia ran back along the beach. Halfway up the stairs she met Alessandra coming down, field glasses in her hands.

'What is it, child? What is wrong? What have you seen?'

'A seal,' said Saskia. 'And I think it is dying. It looks in a terrible state, gasping for breath.'

'What, what?' cried Alessandra.

'A seal,' Saskia repeated. 'At first I thought it was a person, but it is a seal. A very ill seal.'

'A seal!' Alessandra almost shrieked. 'You are sure it is a seal?'

Saskia took a breath. 'Yes,' she said. 'It's not a shark or anything dangerous. It is definitely a seal, and it might be dying.'

Alessandra stared at Saskia as though she still did not understand. 'What can we do? What can we do?'

'Cover it with a rug or a blanket and phone someone,' suggested Saskia. 'Is there an animal rescue centre nearby?' And as Alessandra did not reply she said, 'The local police station would know. We could ask them.'

Alessandra spoke in an odd voice. 'The police,' she said.

'Well, I suppose it's not really an emergency,' said Saskia. 'We could contact the RSPCA or the coastguard, or someone.'

'What?' Alessandra's face had lost all colour. She stared at Saskia and did not move.

'Do you have a phone book?' said Saskia. 'I could look up the number.'

'No. That is, yes.' Alessandra twisted her fingers together. 'Let me . . . let me . . .' she stammered, 'j-just ask N-Neil Buchan. He'll take care of it. Yes,' she repeated, 'Neil will see to it.'

Saskia had a sudden image of Neil putting the seal in a taxi, but then she supposed that if he brought the pick-up truck then it was not too ridiculous. She followed Alessandra as she hurried up the beach stairs and into the house. Why should her great-aunt be so startled by the idea of a seal on the beach?

As if Saskia had voiced her thoughts Alessandra said, 'Fisherfolk have no great love of seals, you know. They tear the nets, and . . . and . . . things like that.'

Once in the house Alessandra found an old tartan travelling rug. 'Be careful.' She held the rug for a moment before handing it to Saskia. 'Be careful on the rocks.'

Saskia took the rug, went back on the beach and draped it over the seal. It hardly moved, only fastened huge blurry eyes on her face and twisted its head this way and that. It seemed to know that she was trying to help it, and became still as she reached up and wrapped the blanket around it and tucked it underneath its body.

'There,' she said, patting it. How did one comfort a seal? She hoped Alessandra had phoned Neil Buchan and he was able to get some kind of help.

They had lunch while they waited. Again Saskia watched as her great-aunt set out the dishes, but Alessandra's careful constrained manner of the morning was shaken.

Her great-aunt stared at the cupboards, concentrating, before opening one and slowly, hesitatingly, bringing out dishes and food. As they sat down to eat Alessandra switched on the radio. The routine of preparing lunch seemed to have calmed her, and her voice was almost even as she said, 'Do you mind my turning this on?' Alessandra pointed to the radio. 'I like to hear the shipping forecast. I suppose you find it a bit boring?'

'I don't know,' said Saskia. 'I've never paid it much attention before. In London if I want to know what the weather is like I just look out of the window.'

The steady beat of the announcer's voice swelled into the kitchen. '*Frontal trough moving steadily south . . . Cromarty, Forth, Tyne: northerly, backing northwest, four or five, occasionally six, showers; mainly good. Dogger: northerly, bearing northeasterly, five or six, decreasing four or five, showers; good. German Bight, Humber, Thames, Dover: northeast, backing north, five or six, wintry showers; moderate or good. Wight, Portland, Plymouth: northeasterly, five to seven, occasionally gale eight, wintry showers; good, occasionally poor. Lundy, Fastnet . . . Shannon . . . Rockall, Malin . . . Hebrides . . . Bailey . . . Faeroes . . . Fair Isle. South-east Iceland: west four or five, showers; moderate or good.*'

They listened in silence to this solemn recitation of the

wind and weather conditions on the seas encircling them. 'I like it,' said Saskia eventually. 'I find it sort of . . . comforting.'

Alessandra looked pleased. 'Yes, that's it,' she said. 'To know that someone somewhere is keeping watch for them, even if it is via satellite or a machine or a computer. It's a long time since I've been involved with bringing in the fish, but everyone in a fishing community is bonded to each other and to the sea.'

'I can appreciate that,' said Saskia. 'I expect that whole villages and towns depend on the boats having good catches.'

'It's not just the economics of it,' said Alessandra. 'It's much more than that. I think it's about us being a sea-faring people. It's what we are . . . No, it's *who* we are.'

'You think we're linked to our landscape?' asked Saskia. She thought of the people she had met during her time in the remote parts of Asia, how integrated they seemed to be with their country, even down to how they looked and dressed.

'Do *you* think we are?' Alessandra smiled. 'Where do our stories and customs come from? There are so many inspired by this area alone that they would fill more books than one person could ever write.'

'My dad says that fisherfolk are very superstitious.'

'He's right, although much more so in the past than now. There were so many things that you should or should not do, especially when the boats were about to sail. My own mother died when I was quite young but I do remember her baiting the hooks for the line fishing. She always began the work on a Tuesday and no one was allowed to enter the house without them baiting a few of the hooks. At New Year we took salt water from the sea and sprinkled it on our hearth. We gathered seaweed from the shore and placed it over the doors.'

They were so caught up in the conversation, Alessandra retelling the old ways that she could remember, Saskia listening intently, that both of them were startled when the heavy brass knocker sounded on the front door.

Saskia went to open the door with Alessandra following anxiously behind her. Despite being fairly tall herself, Saskia found she had to look up to meet the eyes of the young man who stood there.

'Ben Nicholson,' he said, smiling. 'I'm from the local Marine Research Station. You reported a seal in trouble on the beach?'

'Right,' Saskia replied, suddenly aware that her hair was messy, her clothes were scruffy, she had no make-up on, and that as well as being tall, this man was extremely good looking. Dark hair, dark eyes, and the kind of tanned skin that indicated a life spent working outside. 'Right,' she repeated.

Ben grinned and looked from Alessandra to Saskia. 'You wouldn't like to point out where exactly?'

Saskia felt her face colour. 'Of course,' she said. She led him to the top of the beach stairs and indicated the other end of the beach.

'I've got a stretcher in my van.' Ben looked at the stairs and then turned and looked Saskia up and down. 'I'm wondering if you'd be able to manage to carry the animal up these stairs with me?'

Saskia's face began to colour up again, and as it did, Ben spoke at once. 'Look, no offence, but seals can be quite heavy animals. Was it a full-grown male?'

'I haven't a clue,' said Saskia. She met his eyes and this time held his gaze. 'I'm prepared to give it a try though.'

'Good for you,' said Ben. 'Let's get the gear out of the van. I parked it on the top road.'

As she followed Ben, Saskia pulled a scrunchie from her pocket and quickly tied her hair back.

'This is a fantastic little cove,' said Ben, 'and the house is brilliant. Have you lived here long?'

'I'm on holiday for a bit, but my great-aunt has lived here all her life.'

Ben grinned again. 'Actually I could tell by your accent that you're not local. I was just being nosy.'

'So, where are you from?' asked Saskia. 'I can tell by your accent that you *are* local.'

'Ah,' said Ben. 'The locals in this part of the world wouldn't agree with you. This part of the Northeast from below Peterhead and up beyond Fraserburgh is known as Buchan country and I'm from further south, St Andrews. The accent and even the language are different here.'

'Oh, yes,' said Saskia. 'My great-aunt said they speak Doric here.'

'*The* Doric,' said Ben. 'Far'r ye fae?'

'Translate please,' laughed Saskia.

'Where are you from?'

'London,' said Saskia. 'Although my grandfather was my great-aunt's brother and my father was born in Cliff House just after the Second World War.'

'So you're more of a local than I am,' said Ben. 'Here, grab an end of this.' He pulled a large canvas and aluminium stretcher from the van, and then a rucksack.

As they walked down the beach stairs carrying the stretcher together, Saskia saw what looked like a rifle poking out of the top. 'You're not going to kill it, are you?'

'It might need sedating to get it onto the stretcher, but, yes' – he turned and regarded her seriously – 'it might be that it has to be put down.'

'I thought you were supposed to save sick animals.' Saskia could not keep the disappointment from her voice.

'First of all, I'm not from the RSPCA. I'm from a Marine Research Institute,' said Ben. 'And also we think that there's some kind of seal flu on its way here so we're trying to contain it. We don't know enough about it yet to have any treatment for them, but what we do know is that seals gather together in colonies and they also swim huge distances in search of food so it could easily become an epidemic. There's a special crematorium being set up in Inverness. If we can bring them in and burn the bodies then we might be able to hold it up, at least until after the seal pups are born later in the year.'

'It seems an awful thing to do,' said Saskia as they began to walk along the beach.

'It's a sleep dart. The least cruel way we know. Honestly,' Ben added. 'It has to be better than leaving it to suffer.'

Saskia took Ben to the place at the far end of the beach where she had found the stricken animal. They stood and looked up at the big flat rock where Saskia had found the seal.

There was nothing there. Not even the rug. The rock was empty. The seal had gone.

Chapter 9

'Perhaps it wasn't in as much distress as you imagined,' said Ben.

'I didn't *imagine* it,' said Saskia. 'I saw it lying right there, and it was very ill indeed.'

'OK, OK,' said Ben, looking around. 'It's not on the beach so it must have gone back into the sea.' He took field glasses from his rucksack and began to scan the water near the shore.

'I wouldn't have thought it capable of doing that,' said Saskia.

'If it was in the condition you described then you are right, it wouldn't be able to dive properly,' said Ben. 'The very ill ones that have been picked up so far have had advanced emphysema and they don't want to go into the water, but' – he took his eyes from his field glasses and looked along the beach – 'I don't see where else it could have gone.'

'I suppose it could have fallen off the rock,' said Saskia.

'And then been swept out to sea? It's a possibility,' Ben replied. He began to scan the water.

Saskia looked more intently at the rocks. 'It might have

crawled off deeper into these rocks for shelter. Further round this bit of headland.'

Ben clambered on top of the nearest one. 'There doesn't seem to be a way through here.' He jumped back down onto the sand beside her.

'My great-aunt says these rocks are dangerous.' Saskia hesitated. 'Do you think they are?'

'Never ignore local knowledge,' said Ben. 'Your aunt will know more about the conditions here than you or I ever will. The water swirling around this little headland looks treacherous, and if a boat struck on them, there doesn't seem to be anything a person could cling on to.'

'Yes, but she doesn't like me going anywhere near them even from the shore side. I mean, for a walker on the beach, they can't be dangerous,' Saskia persisted.

'It might be that there was a fatal accident here in the dim and distant past, say a child killed or something similar. That can be why people tell you to avoid certain places. Over time it becomes a local story but no one can remember why there's bad luck connected with a particular place, although originally there is a good reason for the warning.'

Saskia looked at the headland again. Alessandra was uncomfortable about this part of the beach. Had Ben's explanation any truth in it?

'I'd say you'd need climbing gear to get over these rocks safely,' Ben went on, 'so I'm definitely not risking it. The current's probably deadly when the tide turns. If you slipped you'd get caught, and nothing would save you from being dragged down.'

As they went back along the beach Ben looked up at

the house. 'It's very impressive,' he said. 'Quite a few houses by the sea in the Northeast are built like that, gable end to the sea and the doors facing inland, but I've never seen one so deeply set into the cliff.'

Alessandra was waiting at the top of the stairs. Saskia suddenly recalled that when her great-aunt had run to meet her on the stairs Alessandra had been carrying her old-fashioned binoculars. She was carrying them now.

'The seal is gone,' said Saskia. 'Did you see what happened to it?'

'No, no,' said Alessandra. 'How would I see anything?'

'Earlier, when I found the seal, you had your binoculars on me.'

Alessandra's face showed upset. 'It was only to make sure that you were all right.'

'But you *were* watching the beach.'

'The . . . the . . . rocks are dangerous. I was afraid for you.'

Saskia was becoming irritated and it was threatening to overcome her good manners. 'Aunt Alessandra!' she said sharply. 'Were you watching just now? Did you see the seal move away as Ben and I approached it?'

'Moved away,' Alessandra repeated. 'Yes. I-i-it moved – t-t-to the water. I think. There were other seals swimming there.'

Saskia glanced at Ben and saw a curious look on his face and her annoyance began to extend to him. Impatiently she snapped, 'I *did* see a seal, you know. And it was very ill.'

'I believe you,' said Ben in a neutral tone of voice. 'If it saw other seals out in the water it would give it the motivation to go and join them. Initially, they might have moved from the rocks into the water and away from it when they saw that it was unwell.'

Saskia realized that she was sounding a bit neurotic. She'd have to calm down. *Doucement, doucement,* she told herself, and then was horribly aware that she was using the words her mother sometimes muttered under her breath when her father was about to lose his temper.

'I'm sorry,' she said to both Ben and Alessandra. 'I got a bit stressed. The poor animal looked as though it was dying.'

'It's very hard when you see a creature in distress and you can't do anything to help it,' said Ben. He held up his hands, which were covered in sand. 'Is there anywhere I could wash my hands?'

'Of course,' said Saskia. 'I'll make us all some coffee while you do that.'

Now Alessandra became even more flustered and Saskia suddenly felt bad about that. She had come barging into her great-aunt's quiet and ordered life, urged on by her father for his own interests, and had managed within the space of a day to destroy Alessandra's tranquillity.

Neil Buchan arrived just as they were going indoors. He spoke directly to Alessandra. 'I got here as soon as I could.' He then introduced himself to Ben.

Saskia had the impression that her great-aunt had not had so many people in her kitchen for a very long time. Alessandra was agitated, pulling open cupboards at random, searching for extra mugs. 'You sit down, Alessandra,' said Saskia. 'I'll make the coffee.'

Neil had his eyes on Alessandra's face. 'Yer all right.'

Saskia glanced at him, surprised at the tone of his voice. He was not asking Alessandra how she was. He was telling her something.

'There is nothing on the beach,' he spoke quietly. 'Everything is fine. Yer all right,' he said again.

'Yes?' Alessandra looked into his face, and then down at her hands. She clenched them tightly in front of her. 'Yes.'

Ben was chatting away easily, unaware of any tension in the room, and Saskia found herself responding to him. He must be in his early twenties, she guessed. He had just finished a degree in marine biology, working at the famous Gatty Laboratory of St Andrews University, and was now doing post-graduate research at the Marine Institute in Aberdeen.

'I happened to be at the Marine Research Station on the other side of Fhindhaven when your call came in so they asked me to come and investigate.'

Neil gave him a searching look. 'Are ye one o' those laboratory scientists that ken more about fish than fishermen?'

Ben sipped his coffee, then he raised his head and stared directly at Neil. 'Yes,' he said. 'In some cases I think I do.'

Saskia drew in her breath. Such a flash of arrogance to put her off, just when she thought he seemed quite nice to get to know.

'I've fished as far north as Greenland and right up into the Barents Sea,' Ben went on without rancour, 'but I reckon I've learned a lot from books and scientific research that I wouldn't have known from only being at sea.'

'And would that work the ither way then?' said Neil, standing his ground.

'It would,' said Ben.

'Seals aren't fish anyway,' interrupted Saskia.

'No,' said Ben, 'but they are part of the life system. And each creature on this planet is connected to the other.'

'There's few fishermen would grieve a seal's death,' said Neil. 'They devour so mony fish.'

Ben raised his eyebrows. 'Don't we?'

Neil laughed. 'Ach well,' he said. 'I'm fae the old school who believe that man has more rights than animals.'

'But with that right comes responsibility, surely,' said Ben.

Saskia glanced at him. The look on his face was intense. He obviously cared deeply about his work.

'There isn't an inexhaustible supply of fish in the sea,' Ben went on. 'If we don't formulate some policies on conservation, then the time might come when we have to close our fishing grounds.'

'That could never happen!' Saskia looked from one to the other. 'Could it?'

'They're talking about it in Canada,' said Ben. 'They say they'll close the Grand Banks in a couple of years.'

'The herring a' all but gone fae the North Sea,' said Neil. 'And when I was young nae body would ever have foreseen that day.'

'I think sometimes we leave taking action until it's too late,' said Ben.

'The restrictions and regulations that've been already laid doon are worse than useless,' said Neil. 'When we went into Europe the fact sheets issued by oor own government said that they would prevent anything which ran counter to oor major national interest. But the Common Fisheries Policy disnae tak' into account that this is the only livelihood for the British coastal communities from Cornwall to the Shetlands. The Icelanders were smart enough tae extend their exclusion zone. But then nae every other nation will agree to another's wishes.'

Ben nodded. 'That's a major part of the issue, but much more than protection of self-interest is at stake here. It's important for all concerned to be aware of the consequences of modern fishing methods.'

'The men's safety should come first,' said Neil.

'Conservation measures don't have to compromise safety!' Ben said passionately. 'We must pay attention to scientific findings. And scientists need to make their information available to all. It's the reason I went into marine research. The more we know about life in the sea the more we can work towards preserving it – for everybody's benefit.'

'Is that why you're out rescuing seals?' asked Saskia.

'We're only lending a hand at the moment,' said Ben. 'Reports are coming in of dead seals from as far north as the Orkneys. Norfolk and the Moray Firth are seeing the worst of it, but the whole seal population is threatened. We think it began on Anholt, which lies between

Denmark and Sweden, but it's spreading rapidly. Seals are very gregarious and regularly travel long distances, so it arrived here in a space of weeks. Scotland has most of the United Kingdom's seal population, and the majority of the Atlantic grey seals live in Scottish waters so there are not enough staff in our animal rescue centres to cope. The scientists think it might be a virus, some kind of distemper, but it's not one they are familiar with.' He stood up. 'I'll have to go.' He went over to Alessandra and touched her gently on the shoulder. 'Don't worry about it,' he said gently. 'It's not contagious to humans. If you see another one, you don't have to go near it. Just contact us and we'll deal with it.' He wrote out his phone number and office address in Aberdeen.

He spoke to Saskia as she helped him carry the stretcher back to his van. 'Are you planning to do anything special during your time here?'

'Not really.' She shrugged. 'I'll probably help my great-aunt. She's doing historical research and I've said I might do some typing for her.'

'If you get bored you can give me a call,' said Ben. He smiled at Saskia. 'Even if you don't find that seal again.'

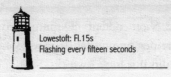

Lowestoft: Fl.15s
Flashing every fifteen seconds

Chapter 10

After dinner, Saskia tried telephoning her parents again. This time she put the receiver down as soon as the answering machine came on. Her aunt looked up from the book she was reading as Saskia returned to the living room. 'There wouldn't be anything wrong?'

'Oh, no,' said Saskia. 'They go out a lot.' She didn't add 'but not together' as she might have done if it was one of her friends. 'That long journey yesterday has caught up with me,' she continued. 'I thought I might have a bath and go to bed early. I brought a stereo and tapes with me. Do you mind if I play my music?'

'Not at all.' Alessandra paused for a second. 'As long as you don't mind if I play mine.'

It was a joke. Her aunt had made a joke. Saskia stared, smiled, and then laughed.

It was as if something unheard of and very unusual had happened, but now Alessandra was unsure how to proceed or how to act or react. She studied Saskia for a moment and then said, 'You must find me a very strange person.'

'Not really,' Saskia replied automatically. She

shrugged and then added. 'Define "strange". What's normal for one person can be strange to another.'

Alessandra did not look away.

'OK,' said Saskia. 'A bit.'

Alessandra smiled. 'How honest is youth.'

'You mean cheeky,' Saskia joked back.

'No, I don't think I do,' said Alessandra. 'It's . . . refreshing, yes, I think that's what I mean, refreshing. Certainly it is preferable to have someone say things *to* you than talk badly of you behind your back.'

Saskia didn't reply. Did Alessandra mean her father? How could she possibly know how he spoke of her to Saskia?

'You probably heard Neil reassuring me in the kitchen earlier that everything was all right.' Alessandra spoke slowly. 'I . . . I . . . I was troubled with my nerves for a long while, and he knows that I become agitated . . . about certain things. Tragedy touched my life . . . such a weight of sadness to carry, it almost overwhelmed me. I've got tablets . . . now. Although sometimes I forget to take them. That's why I said to you this morning that I might not remember if I was up and about last night.' She paused and then said, 'I used to sleepwalk.'

'How awful,' said Saskia. 'One of the girls in my year group used to do that. She would wake up outside in the garden and have no idea how she got there.'

'Yes,' said Alessandra slowly. 'I found myself on the beach a few times. I imagined I saw things . . . people . . . my family, the ones who had died. I would wake up by the water's edge. Not safe . . . It was years ago but I got a name in the village for being odd. That sort of thing

70

sticks. And when one person thinks a thing, then others join in for reasons of their own or . . . sometimes for no reason.'

'People do that,' said Saskia, memories of incidents at school surfacing in her mind. Of fellow pupils ganging up against each other.

'I found that if you smile at the wrong places or laugh inappropriately it unnerves people,' Alessandra went on. 'The pills the doctor gave me disorientated me. I felt detached from the world. I laughed frequently.'

'It's good to laugh,' said Saskia.

'Not at funerals,' said Alessandra. 'I had to stop going to church. Everything the minister said gave me cause to smile. I found some Bible readings hilarious.'

'So?' said Saskia loyally. 'They should have been glad to see you happy after suffering such grief.'

'Not during church services,' said Alessandra. 'I found that even the most liberal-minded of the congregation took exception to my giggling during a serious sermon. And it was difficult for the minister. He thought I mocked God.'

'But you got better?' said Saskia.

'I was in hospital for a while. Then . . . then, they let me come home. I was by myself in the house and to begin with I found that I could not leave it. Even now I don't like to be away from the house for long. Recently I made a huge effort to break free and take part in the Heritage Project. It was an act of kindness by a cousin of Neil Buchan. She persuaded me to volunteer. She said I would like the work, that I needed company now that you and your father and mother no longer came. I think

Neil told her that I was on my own too much. First they asked me if I had any old photographs that were suitable for copying, and then she asked me to do one or two other things, and now I work part-time for them. To begin with it was difficult for me . . . to interact with people again, but I found that I liked taping the reminiscences of the older men and women. At first I just went to those I knew from when I was a young woman. They were very kind. I didn't need to do or say very much, just switch the tape recorder on and off. Then the Heritage Centre gave me a camera and a tape recorder to work on my own at home. I only need to go into the centre one day a week. They pay me a small wage and an allowance for expenses and . . . and . . . I actually enjoy doing it.'

Her great-aunt's conversation was in Saskia's mind as she bathed and washed the grit and sand from her hair before going to bed that night. Alessandra's account of her depression explained a lot about her behaviour. Saskia guessed that any type of mental illness would shake a person's confidence, and would make it more difficult for them to be in company. And of course people were uncomfortable with anyone who was 'different' – which, within a community, could result in that person being isolated, even picked on.

It wasn't so long since Saskia had been through those years at school when having a friend or being part of a group was almost essential to survive. She knew how easy it was for the outsider to be pushed further and further away. She thought again of the fish in the sea and how they react to any subtle change within their environment. How fish swim in shoals, and respond to urges. The salmon travelling hundreds and hundreds of miles to return to their own spawning ground, the eels' pilgrimage to the Sargasso Sea. People seemed driven by basic instincts, flitting away from anything that might seem like danger. Moving as one to shun the perceived enemy; getting caught up in gang behaviour, like crowds who turn up to kick police vans and shout abuse at those arrested for murder when they don't know for sure if the accused is guilty or not.

Yet it was easy for an individual to be sucked in. Saskia became uncomfortable as her thoughts progressed . . . the shame still with her at being one of those who had joined in a bullying episode at school some years ago: name calling, cold-shouldering the girl whose turn it was to be left out. The whole incident had lasted several weeks. Days of mounting tension, personal and communal. Saskia's helpless feeling at being dragged in, horrified by her own actions at the time, but seemingly not able to stop herself.

She bent her head as she relived her mixed confusion of emotions – self-disgust, with a horrible moment of slithering pleasure on seeing the victim, Emma, break down weeping. Shock that some of the boys in her class had also contributed to the ugliness, adding their own vocabulary of abuse, hurling words like 'cow' and 'slag' at Emma.

Eventually the school had taken action, changing Emma's classes, the guidance teacher spending a morning lecturing the whole year group. Afterwards Saskia found she was not able to look at her friends directly or talk about her own behaviour with anyone. Their different reactions confused her. Some dismissed the whole incident and moved on, sloughing it off with no remorse. Others argued that Emma had deserved it, had it coming, or that it was just part of life – you just had to learn to take it. A few, like Saskia herself, were embarrassed and did not take part in any of the discussions.

Saskia was sure Emma had been altered for the better by the experience. Although terribly hurt, Emma had evolved stronger, whereas Saskia had felt that she herself had been damaged and, for her, the outcome had been less positive. She'd found it difficult to live with herself for months afterwards. That she could have been so weak! Had so little confidence that she'd gone along with it all. And those excuses she had made for herself at the time that she had trouble at home just did not wash – everyone had trouble at home.

The Head had moved Emma into different subject classes and out of their class for English and Maths into the year ahead. It must have been tough going, making new friends under duress and taking key subjects at a faster pace than she could really cope with. But Saskia had bumped into Emma leaving school one day almost a year later, and Emma had said 'Hi'. Emma had made this first move. Saskia had been too ashamed to say much in reply, couldn't believe that Emma had not borne her a grudge. The same Saskia who had stood and watched Emma's lunch box being opened up, the contents thrown away and replaced with earth. The same

Saskia who had obeyed the order of the leader of the bullies; at the queen bee's command she had brought Emma's school bag to them so that they could do the deed. And Emma must have known that. She had left her school bag beside Saskia in the cloakroom when she went off to the loo.

After all that, Emma had said . . .

'Hi! How are you?'

'Erm . . . fine,' Saskia had managed a smile. 'How are you?'

'Working like crazy,' Emma had replied, 'trying to keep up with the rest of them in this new class I've been put into. You know me. I never was very academic, but I'm actually enjoying it and I'm attempting things I'd never have believed I was capable of doing.'

Saskia had seen Emma later at the local cinema with a group of older pupils, talking and laughing. One of the boys had had his arm around her. Saskia had accepted that her own fleeting moment of jealousy was deserved. Emma had outgrown them all, become more mature, with no residue of bitterness, and Saskia realized that she'd lost a potential good friend.

Good grief! She should be studying psychology instead of accounts. Saskia brushed out her hair quickly. The water was much softer here than in London and her hair had changed texture, become more difficult to manage. Little tendrils coiled round her face. When she looked in the mirror she could see no resemblance to Alessandra, or indeed to any of the Granton side of her family, apart from the dark reddish sheen to her hair. It had begun to lighten in the sun, that hard unforgiving light of early spring that caught you unexpectedly, reflecting angles of the windows within the house. It showed up the hall and its varnished wallpaper with its scrolled, embossed design, a style so old that it was almost fashionable again. Picking out the worn parts and faded marks on the carpet. The shadows on those outside stairs recessed into the wall, the shaft of light catching the line of the harpoon, dark rust spreading on its tip. Her mother had always said Saskia had an eye for colour, even from when she was very young. All the hues of Cliff House and the bay were imprinted on her eyes. London so distant now, city tones so different.

Already her face was burnished across nose and forehead; her skin singing with the wind and the sea spray. Saskia lay down on her bed to listen to her tapes, then switched off her stereo and listened instead to the ebb tide rustling its skirts below her window.

Over the surface of the sea drift vast expanses of plankton. Within this ceaseless moving phosphorescent mass lie the vital micro-organisms of life, spreading a food web for all the world.

Chapter 11

Saskia's father phoned the next morning.

'How are you, darling? Sorry neither of us got back to you the first night when you phoned. We were both out, and then I got a bit tied up with things yesterday so I didn't get a chance to call you until now. Anyway,' he went on without giving Saskia a chance to speak, 'how is Alessandra?'

'She's fine,' said Saskia.

'Her manner can be a bit peculiar at times, but that's just Alessandra's way. So . . . everything is OK?'

'Yes,' said Saskia, 'although we had a bit of excitement yesterday. There was a seal in trouble on the beach and someone came along to try to rescue it but it had disappeared.'

'How was she with that?' asked Saskia's father. 'She's not used to strangers in her house. Apart from us, the only person who used to visit was a chap who grew up with her, a Ned or Nick Buchanan or some name like that.'

'Neil Buchan,' said Saskia. 'Yes, I've met him. Well, as I said, it was a bit of excitement at the time, but everything is back to normal now. Aunt Alessandra is doing some work for the local Heritage Centre so I'm going to help her with that.'

'Then you're getting on all right together?' Her father's voice was warmer and Saskia felt happier.

'Yes we are, and the place is wonderful.'

'It is quite a setting,' her father agreed.

'But, Dad,' Saskia said quickly, 'I didn't realize that I had been here when I was a little girl.'

'We spent one or two summers at Cliff House when you were very young, but it was so long ago that you probably don't remember much about it.'

'Why didn't you mention that to me before?'

'Listen, pet, I'm on my way out to meet a prospective client at the moment. I just thought I'd give you a quick call.'

'Hang on, Dad. Before you go, another thing – I thought you told me that Aunt Alessandra asked me to come up here?'

'Yes, that's right.'

'But *she* says . . .' Saskia hesitated. What *had* her aunt said?

'What?' her father asked impatiently.

Saskia lowered her voice, suddenly conscious that she was talking on the phone in the hall and the doors to the other rooms were open. 'Aunt Alessandra said that you told her that it was *me* who asked to visit *her*.'

Saskia's father gave a short laugh. 'She gets things mixed up a bit, you know. I'd better go now. Take care.'

Saskia frowned at the receiver before replacing it. Her father's answers didn't enlighten her at all. The subject was still niggling her later in the day when she was helping her aunt label the fisherfolk interview tapes, so much so that she suddenly decided that she had to find out.

'Aunt Alessandra, I'd like to ask you something.'

'Yes?'

'Did you invite me here to visit you?'

'Saskia, my dear, you are always welcome to stay here.'

'I mean specifically, this year, at this time?'

'Not specifically, no.'

'My father said you asked me to come with my bicycle.'

'Ah yes,' said Alessandra. 'When your father called me and said that you wanted to visit me before going to university, I suggested that you bring your bicycle. There are some very good cycling routes around the coast.'

Saskia spoke briskly. 'Actually, Daddy says that *you* particularly wanted me to visit you just now.'

Alessandra blinked. 'Did he? Did I? I'm sorry. I thought he said, I mean . . .'

Her great-aunt's confusion made Saskia feel juvenile and stupid. She'd upset Alessandra, and for what? Why did it seem important to her that the distinction was made?

Alessandra was watching her anxiously, but recovered herself enough to speak more calmly. 'Does it matter? It was probably a combination of both. I often wrote to ask you all to spend the summer; it was a standing invitation, that's what he probably meant.'

'You wrote? When?'

'Late June, just before your summer holidays, every year.'

Every year!

That's not what her father had said at all. Maybe he was right and Alessandra was losing it – well, getting mixed up at any rate.

'But you know you are welcome,' Alessandra went on. 'At any time, Saskia. Always. Always.'

Alessandra wrote every year?

Her father had implied that they hadn't been in touch for ages. Saskia decided that she would speak to her mother next time she phoned home. And she'd try to do it from a call box in the village. It would be easier than talking with her great-aunt in the house. She would prefer privacy to discuss with her mother her summers here as a child. It was troubling her that her memories of this place seemed shadowed in some way. She had memories of lots of things from when she was small – buying new shoes, birthday parties – why not any from here, especially if they had visited more than once? Had she blocked any thoughts of her times at Cliff House because she believed that Alessandra had fallen out with her father and had never asked them to return? But then why hadn't she recalled even doing that? Was it an inherited family failing? Was she copying a behaviour pattern from her father, who would dismiss a thing if he couldn't deal with – put it aside, act as if it hadn't happened, and be genuinely surprised when faced with it?

With an effort Saskia pulled her mind away from the subject. One of the reasons she had agreed to visit her great-aunt was to escape the tensions within her own home. There was no point in travelling all this way and then spending her time brooding over her parents' behaviour. She thought about Ben's offer to give him a call. It would be good to get out with different company, perhaps see more of the countryside. But in any case, tomorrow or the next day she'd make some excuse to go into Fhindhaven and she'd phone home from there.

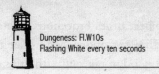

Dungeness: Fl.W10s
Flashing White every ten seconds

Chapter 12

It was the end of the week before Saskia eventually walked into Fhindhaven.

On the afternoon of the day her father phoned, the weather changed and a storm came in with frightening speed. Saskia stood with Alessandra at the drawing-room windows and watched huge breaking waves running into the cove. The sea dashed against the cliff face, surging high into the many fissures and clefts and then swirling back, foam hissing between the rocks. Great clouds banked on the eastern horizon and the wind shifted round.

'It will be like this for today and tomorrow,' said Alessandra. 'You might not want to go out. It's not so pretty on the beach when there's a gale blowing.'

Saskia gazed out to where sea met sky on a vivid colourist canvas of overlapping purples and greys. 'Not pretty,' she agreed. 'Beautiful.'

For the two days the storm lasted Saskia borrowed a hat and gloves from Alessandra and walked each morning on the beach and along the top road to the cliffs overlooking Fhindhaven. She returned to the house by lunch time, breathless and ravenous. In the afternoons they catalogued the photographs together, old and new, and on Thursday night they laid a fire in the drawing room, and made toast by the hearth. Saskia licked hot butter from her fingers and watched the open flames as her aunt went to make a pot of tea.

This time the memory came complete; the scene playing out in Saskia's head from beginning to end.

Alessandra was singing her a lullaby. Sitting by this very fire with Saskia on her knee, telling her a bedtime story. Saskia squeezed her eyes closed. How old had she been? Four? Five? Saskia remembered her great-aunt's way of speaking. The tales of the north, told in a lilting tongue. Saskia in thrall to the sounds, and the natural power of the story. She hadn't known the meaning of every word Alessandra used, yet only occasionally had she interrupted . . .

'Aunt Alessandra, what's a silkie?'

And Alessandra answers, without interrupting the flow of her story, weaving the explanation into the narrative.

'My child, it's the spirit of the sea. It sometimes takes the form of a seal, though you can always tell in some way if it is not a true seal. The old ones say that the silkies look after the souls of the poor drowned fishermen. They say the silkies catch their bodies as they slide beneath the waves and gently, gently, lower them onto the floor of the ocean. And there the silkies watch over them so that they can rest in peace.'

'Is that what happened to my grandfather? Daddy says his daddy got lost at sea. Did the silkies find him?'

Her great-aunt whispers, 'I hope so. I believe so.' Alessandra bends and kisses Saskia's forehead. 'Hush now, my little quine . . . may hosts of angels lull you to your sleep.'

Saskia opened her eyes. Alessandra had returned. She stood with her eyes on Saskia's face. The fire stretched her shadow on the ceiling. Saskia knew without asking that their thoughts were synchronized.

'The stories you told me . . . Where did they come from?'

'From my mother, and her mother, I expect . . . and so on.'

Saskia knew now that when she was a child her great-aunt had always spoken to her in a different way. As though they shared a secret from her parents, as though Alessandra was, like her at the time, not a grown-up. And now . . . ? And now Saskia was excluded. She was too old to be part of that bonding, the shared secrets of children. It should have amused her or annoyed her, but it didn't. It made her sad. Maybe her great-aunt was right. The reason her parents stopped bringing her to Cliff House was merely because she had grown out of coming here.

By Friday the weather had cleared and Saskia did not need to make an excuse to visit Fhindhaven. Alessandra needed some groceries and was grateful when Saskia offered to shop for her. Coming out of the shop Saskia put her purchases into her rucksack and went to find a call box.

It was her father who answered the phone and when she asked to speak to her mother he said, 'Your mother's gone off for a few days with a couple of artist friends for a so-called painting trip.'

'In that case,' Saskia spoke firmly, 'there's something you could help me get straight.' She was determined that this time she would not have her question sidestepped. 'Dad, Great-aunt Alessandra says that she did not invite me specifically this year, but that she did write to invite us to stay every year for the last ten years or so.'

'Oh, no. No—'

'She doesn't *seem* the type to lie, Dad.'

'Getting old then, losing her mind.'

Saskia hesitated, not wanting to contradict her father twice in as many seconds but knowing that Alessandra had been definite about writing letters of invitation every year.

'She's not senile.'

'Well something like that,' he said irritably.

Saskia found that she was speaking to her father the way that her mother did. Trying to pin him to the truth of a situation when he did not appear himself to know that he was being evasive.

'Did she not write? Not at all? Apart from the letter you showed me?'

'There was another letter, I think.'

'Just one?'

'What?'

'Only one? Did she send only one other letter asking us to visit?'

'There may have more, over the years.'

'Two more? Three? How many?'

'Why are you pursuing this? Does it matter?'

Alessandra had said the same thing. Saskia thought, Why *does* it matter to me? Why was it important?

'It's just that she is insisting on . . .' Saskia searched for a way to please him, to appeal to his own interests. She heard herself lapse into her little girl's voice, almost lisping, and was embarrassed to do it. 'Daddy, I just want to get things clear in my head. She likes talking about the past a lot, and how we played together on the beach when I was small. I thought you wanted me to get to know her better.'

He responded at once. 'Sorry, pet. I *do* want you to be friendly with her. Break the ice a bit. I've got a major project coming off and I was thinking of asking her to invest some money in it. Actually I'd be doing her a bit of a favour. It's a good investment — she'd stand to make a big profit.'

'Well then,' Saskia persisted; 'about these letters?'

He tutted. 'Is she going on about them? Yes, yes, she did write letters every year asking us to come back and stay for the summer, but well, you were growing up, tired of that kind of holiday. We all wanted to go abroad where the weather is more settled, get a bit of sun rather than being stuck in that big old house.'

Saskia held the receiver away from her ear.

He had lied to her.

She could hear his voice, blustering, and then gaining strength as he returned to the subject of his new business venture. Saskia had a vague recollection of this particular project, a leisure complex in southern France. It had cropped up in the more recent rows between him and her mother.

'So, you see, it's really good that Alessandra kept writing to me every year. It meant I knew that she would welcome a visit from you at any time. And you're old enough now to go there on your own so it has worked in very well. She always had a soft spot for you. I'll phone you next week to see if she's ready to talk to me about an investment. You'll be kind and pleasant to her, won't you?'

Saskia mumbled an agreement and then hung up the phone.

Why had her father not told her that Alessandra had written every year to invite them to visit her?

Because if she had known about Alessandra's invitation she might have wanted to spend her summer holidays here.

And, up until now, he had not really wanted her to visit Cliff House. Was it because of his own aversion to the sea? Or more to do with Alessandra and her strange ways? Her dad had said that his aunt was odd. How odd? Odd enough for the family not to continue to visit when she was growing up? Alessandra admitted that she had been unwell for years. She spoke of being prescribed tablets. It must be some kind of sedative that she took. Saskia tried to remember the girl, Jane, who had sleep-walked when she was at school. She had gone into therapy. They had found that some trauma had disturbed her. It had all come to light on a school trip to France. Saskia smiled as she recalled how Jane had tried to take advantage of the situation. In the end the party leader had made it plain that sleepwalking into the boys' bed-rooms was *not* acceptable.

Saskia left the call box and wandered along the main

street. For whatever reason she had been kept away in the past, she was glad she was here now. Despite her great-aunt's strangeness she found that she quite liked her. Alessandra's direct way of looking, her stillness, the manner in which she spoke of this place, the villages, the sea; the way Alessandra's voice became lighter, less flat when she did so, the old words creeping in.

Saskia bought herself a can of juice and went to sit on the harbour wall. Walking on the beach on the other side was someone she recognized. It was Ben.

Chapter 13

'Ben!' called Saskia.

Ben looked round. 'Hello,' he shouted back, and waved her over.

Saskia dropped onto the sand and walked to meet him. He was holding a container in one hand and a small fishing net in the other.

'What have you got there?' Saskia peered into his container.

'*Copepod Calanus.*'

'Sorry?'

'Plankton samples.'

'Is it to do with the seal virus?'

'Not exactly. It's work that was ongoing before. But it may come in useful. There's worldwide investigations being done on marine single-cell organisms. They're known to drift with the currents of the ocean, but different types of plankton have distinct areas where they are able to live. They are extremely sensitive to climate conditions. Keeping an eye on what they are up to gives us indicators as to future biological implications.' He

89

stopped. 'Sorry, I do tend to go on a bit.'

'No, no,' said Saskia. 'I'd like to know more. Really, please finish what you were saying.'

'Well, basically there is a type of plankton usually only found to the southwest of Britain and the European seas, and another species is found in the North Sea and the Atlantic. But now it looks as if their boundaries are shifting. And as plankton is the basis of marine life it might have a huge impact on the fisheries for the future.'

'You mean the actual fish stocks?'

'Yes, and on the way we fish. Fishing methods have become more and more aggressive. The boats scoop up all forms of life; it can be very destructive. Young fish need to feed in order to grow. For instance, trawling by bottom dragging can destroy spawning grounds. We have to ensure that species are not wiped out.'

'What about Neil's argument that humans have to live even at the expense of the fish?'

'Look,' said Ben; 'are you finished with that drink?'

There was some juice left in the can but Saskia had had enough. She nodded.

'Can I throw it away?' he asked her.

'Sure.'

Ben took the can from her hand and tossed it onto the beach. 'There you go,' he said.

'Why did you do that?' Saskia gasped.

'Why not?' Ben asked in mock innocence.

'It's outrageous.'

'Why?'

'Don't be annoying.' Saskia laughed. 'You *know* why. Lots of reasons. It's ugly to look at. It's a pollutant. It's not environmentally friendly. You should tidy your rubbish away.'

'But why?' asked Ben. 'Being tidy doesn't benefit *me*. In fact it's an inconvenience.' He walked over and picked up the can. 'I've got to make an extra effort to find a place to dispose of this properly. Why should I bother?'

'If we don't recycle the world will run out of resources.'

'But not while I'm around.'

'It's for the future,' said Saskia.

'My future is tomorrow,' said Ben. 'It makes absolutely no difference to my quality of life whether that can is on the beach or in the bin.'

'You're depressing me,' said Saskia.

'I don't want to do that,' said Ben, smiling. 'How are you occupying your time anyway?'

'I've been helping my aunt catalogue her research materials. It's actually quite interesting. One of the things she's been doing is to take up-to-date photographs of all the old fishing villages and match them with old photographs of the same place.'

'Is she on the staff of the Heritage Centre?' asked Ben.

'Not full time. It's more like volunteer work.'

Ben looked directly at Saskia. 'We need volunteers for the summer . . . if you're looking to fill up any more of your time.'

'I'm only here for a little while to visit my aunt,' said Saskia, suddenly realizing that she had only intended to stay a maximum of two weeks at Cliff House, and one week was already gone.

'Pity.'

Saskia slid a glance in his direction. Had he meant

anything special by that reply? Was it a pity that there would be one less volunteer because they needed help with the seals, or did he think it a pity that *she* in particular didn't volunteer? Ben bought her ice cream and then offered her a lift back to Cliff House as he was on his way to the fish market at Peterhead.

'More research?' asked Saskia.

'Partly. But also because I love being there. I like talking to the fishermen and the harbour master. They know the conditions at sea better than any satellite monitoring system.' Ben glanced at Saskia. 'You might find that interesting too. Though it's better to go in the early morning when they begin to sell the fish and you can watch the boats coming in from a night at sea.'

'How early?' asked Saskia.

'*Very* early,' said Ben, 'but it's worth it. I've been loads of times but I still get a buzz, especially when the fish auction begins.'

'I'd love to see that,' said Saskia.

'Right,' said Ben, grinning at her. 'That's it settled then. I'll pick you up at half past four tomorrow morning.'

That evening as she made dinner for herself and Alessandra, Saskia thought about her phone conversation with her father. She wanted to tell her great-aunt that she had been right and her father wrong about the circumstances of the invitation to visit Cliff House. But she'd feel awkward doing that, letting Alessandra know that she'd phoned home from the village to discuss it with her father.

And there were still things she wanted to sort out in her

head about the time her family had spent here when she was small. Her vague and disjointed recollections needed clarifying, but she decided she would ask those questions of her mother. She was aware that her father had mixed emotions about the sea, mainly to do with his upbringing in his own mother's little cottage in Yarmouth. Saskia knew this part of her father's story. She'd heard it often. It was a flashpoint between her parents.

Her mother always cast it up to him. 'Call yourself a property developer? If only you'd held onto *that* property when your mother died. Those holiday cottages are fetching a fortune nowadays. We could have sold it or let it.'

'I hated it,' said her father. 'The dark poky little rooms, the stink of fish, the noise, ships hooting, foghorns blasting away, boats coming and going at all hours of the morning, and the absolute dire greyness of it all. It's why I don't understand how she' – and he jabbed his finger at Saskia – 'is so fascinated by the sea. It's cold and cruel and takes lives winter after winter after winter, men dying, women weeping. As well as being widowed by it, my mother lost four brothers.'

'There's no need to carry on so.' Saskia's mother had picked up an emery board and began to file her nails. 'That's all in the past.'

'No it's not in the past!' her father had roared. 'Where do you think the fish comes from that arrives on your plate? Your lemon sole, your baby codling, or prawn cocktails? When you and your figure-conscious friends lunch together they often choose fish, don't they? It's a low-calorie meal for weight-obsessed females.'

'Yes, darling, but it's not actually our *fault* that fishermen have a dangerous occupation.' Her mother raised her eyes to the ceiling and said in a bored, amused voice, 'You have this habit of trying to make someone else feel guilty for your emotional hang-ups. By eating fish you could say that weight-watchers everywhere are actually keeping all those people in a job.'

'It's not funny!'

'I wasn't laughing. Did you see me laughing? Saskia?' Her mother had turned to her. 'Was I laughing?'

Saskia had crept from the room as the argument escalated.

As she and Alessandra ate dinner together that night, Saskia decided to probe a little into her own family history.

'Would you tell me about my grandfather, Alessandra?'

'Rob?' Alessandra said the word slowly, holding her brother's name in her mouth for a moment.

Saskia waited.

Alessandra sighed. 'What would you like to know?'

'Anything,' said Saskia. 'What he looked like, what life was like growing up here. Anything at all.'

'Och, but he was a bonnie boy,' said Alessandra. 'He was two years older than me. A kind brother who grew to be a big handsome fisherlad. We both worked at the fishing from when we were small and he went to sea at fourteen. My father kept creels for partans and lobster, and in the winter Rob went line fishing inshore. He always brought in the best fish. He told me that he found

94

the mark by using Cliff House as his reference point when sailing out.

'That's how he knew where to fish?' asked Saskia.

Alessandra nodded. 'I'd collect mussels among the rocks and bait the lines for him. It was wartime and the deep-sea fishing was restricted, although some boats did go out. The Royal Navy was sent to protect them but they had enough on their hands trying to guard the merchant convoys across the Atlantic. Then after the war, when the season began, Rob went with the other young lads to follow the herring. I remember sitting in front of the house with the bone needles, mending his net. Each fisherman brought his own net to the boat. But I wasn't allowed to go with him to the harbour the way the other women and children went to see their men off.'

'Why not?'

Alessandra smiled. 'My hair.' She leaned across and rested her hand gently on Saskia's head. 'More fiery red, a bit like yours, when I was younger. Another superstition: meeting a red-haired person before sailing was bad luck.'

'So you both lived here quite happily with your parents?'

'Not so happily as we might have,' said Alessandra. 'Our mother died when I was eleven and my father suffered from black rages and deemed it fit to vent his temper upon his children. My brother was more biddable than I, and quarrelled less with him. I resented my father's domination of our lives. He did not welcome visitors, did not let us meet with friends in the village. We existed to work for him, not to enjoy ourselves. As we got older I would disobey him. I loved company so much that I didn't care what punishment he gave me, until . . .' Alessandra paused; 'until . . . he found the most cruel way to deal with me. For every misdemeanour of mine, he would beat Rob.'

Saskia nearly dropped the glass she was holding. 'How awful!' she cried.

'It was clever and effective,' said Alessandra.

Saskia thought of her mother, years ago, when Saskia had mentioned that she was thinking of studying biology at school. 'That won't please your father,' her mother had commented. Did all parents emotionally manipulate their children?

'Those were different days,' said Alessandra. 'It is not so long since women and children were considered to be part of a man's property. But anyway, when I was fifteen I could go to the gutting with the other quines. During the year the herring moved all the way down the east coast, beginning in the spring when the fish lay off the Shetland Islands. By autumn they'd reach English waters. The fishing fleets would follow the shoals as they migrated. From all over the Northeast the girls would go in droves to the ports where their men's boats would land their catch. At first my father refused to let me go. He knew that the hours the girls had to work kept them busy, but I would be away from home, and he did not want me to have any freedom at all. However, his greed for money won out, although the wages were not high. I was unskilled and I feared I would not get taken on. But May and Chris, Neil Buchan's two sisters, taught me how to pack. They were older than me, and good teachers. I was hopeless with the knife but I learned to pack the barrels. And so in nineteen forty-six, for the first fishing after the war, off we went, following the boats down the coast to Yarmouth.'

Saskia heard her aunt's voice lighten.

'Now, what I didn't know was that my brother Rob, your grandfather, had met a girl some time previously when his boat had put in at Yarmouth, and he had more than fishing on his mind that year. When we met up in Yarmouth town he told me his secret and it was there that I first met your grandmother Esther, who agreed to marry him. And the next year when Rob came home in the autumn, his boat had the red, white and blue banner of the wedding flag tied to the mast to show that there was a bridegroom aboard.'

'How romantic,' said Saskia. She imagined her grandfather returning proudly to his own village at the end of the fishing season boasting about his bride, and being teased by his shipmates.

'My father was furious of course,' Alessandra went on. 'He could not believe that the son he had thought cowed would even contemplate such a wilful thing. He raged for days about it, but in the end there was nothing he could do.'

'Rob must have loved her very much,' said Saskia. 'That would have given him the courage to stand up to your father.'

'He did,' said Alessandra. 'And Esther was not without her own kind of strength, for at breakfast one morning she calmly announced that if her presence was unwelcome in this house then she'd take her leave and go back home to Yarmouth, and she'd bring myself and Rob with her.'

'Good for her,' commented Saskia, proud that her grandmother was brave enough to speak up for herself.

'But in truth Esther could not have done this,' said Alessandra, 'for her mother was a widow woman and the house overcrowded with children, but my father did not know this. He saw only that he might lose his workers so he stopped ranting for a while.

'So, despite his ill will, we lived together happily, and by the year after they were married Esther was pregnant, and my brother was like a cat with two tails. Late in nineteen forty-seven there were great snow drifts between the villages, but by walking linked together we managed to struggle through to visit the Buchans on the top road and they us. And we talked and told stories and sang that bleak winter away. And my father's dark moods and violent rages did not stop us.'

Saskia had a picture in her mind of Cliff House covered in sparkling snow and the young men and women of the two families, Alessandra, Rob and Esther, with Neil Buchan and his sisters, gathered round the fire singing and laughing together.

'There weren't many luxuries at that time, though, were there?' she asked.

'You don't miss what you've never had,' said Alessandra. 'And there was no television or glossy magazines to make us discontented.' She paused. 'This house has not changed very much since then.'

Except for the company, thought Saskia. It must have

been crowded and noisy; now it was subdued. She wondered if the house itself felt its loss.

'The thaw came,' Alessandra went on, 'and with it, spring. Early in nineteen forty-eight Rob went away to the fishing again. On the day of his departure Esther was so sad she did not leave the house, so it was I who walked part of the way into Fhindhaven with him to bid him farewell.

' "By the time I come home I'll be a father, Alessandra," he said to me. There was wonder in his voice. "Can you believe that? Me, a father?"

'I remember now, I pushed him across the road in fun. "Nae," I said. "*Ye* canna be a father. Ye widna ken how. Whit wid ye dae if the bairn began tae greet?"

'And he laughed and said he'd call for me because I was a canny quine and I'd know what to do.'

Alessandra had put down her knife and fork and Saskia saw that her food was getting cold but she did not interrupt.

'Esther and Rob's baby was born a little early, and came so quickly that we couldn't get the midwife in time. Considering neither Esther nor I were quite sure of what was happening we did very well. Your grandmother was wonderful. She battled through her time with fortitude and your father arrived early in the morning, red in the face and crying his lungs out.

'And then . . .'

Alessandra stopped speaking. Saskia saw within her great-aunt the terrible calmness of great grief. She wanted to tell Alessandra not to continue if it was too distressing but found she could not speak.

'And then,' Alessandra continued quietly, 'we waited for Rob to come home and see his baby son. Every morning we'd go to the windows in the big room at the front of the house to watch for the boats rounding the point towards the harbour at Fhindhaven. But he never came back. His boat returned all right. We saw it approaching from the headland, past the black rocks there, and we stood on the beach steps and waved a tablecloth between us, and Esther held the baby up high. And we were so happy and bursting with pride and excited to think how he'd be when he first saw his son and held him in his arms.'

Alessandra's voice faltered.

'But it was the mission man, not Rob, who walked up the road from Fhindhaven that day. One of the villagers from the Seafarers Mission came to tell us that Rob had been washed overboard. Him and another Fhindhaven man lost their lives that season.'

Sadness was thick within the room. Saskia blinked away tears.

'At first I thought your grandmother was going to die of grief,' said Alessandra. 'And I thought my own heart would break too, but I remembered my promise to my brother so I put my own feelings aside and fought hard to win her back. The baby helped, he demanded attention, and when the time came for your father to be christened his mother called him Alexander.' Alessandra raised her head and looked at Saskia. 'Esther named her and Rob's baby for me, because she said that without me, neither of them would have remained alive.'

'So you and my father have a strong bond between

you,' said Saskia. 'Does he know that part of his family story?'

Alessandra shrugged. 'I don't know. We have never discussed it. His mother may have told him.'

'My grandmother Granton,' said Saskia. 'I don't remember her. She died when I was small.'

'She was most beautiful. And gentle.'

'Why did they go away to live in Yarmouth?'

There was a silence in the room. Alessandra spoke eventually. 'She was frail . . . The winters here are very bad. Her health was poor, her chest . . .'

That night in bed Saskia read for a while and then lay down, her thoughts drifting into half-remembered places. The conversation with her father earlier in the day had upset her more deeply than she had at first realized. Greater even than the knowledge that he had lied to her was her disquiet over the unexplained reason why she could not remember her holidays here, and why they had suddenly been curtailed. Saskia sat up in bed and, as she leaned over to switch on the bedside lamp, she felt her mind rock and a small taste of queasiness crept into her mouth.

She is on the train.

The movement is like the sea, rocking her, swaying back and forth. She pretends she is on a boat. They are going home, home from a holiday in Cliff House. Her favourite place in all the world.

She tells Daddy, 'It's my favourite place in all the world.'

Her saying this annoys her father. She cannot understand why.

'Mummy, why is Daddy angry?'

'Why don't you ask him?'

'Why are you angry, Daddy?'

Her mother's voice, sugar-sweet. 'Perhaps his hand is sore.'

He glares at her mother. 'I think it's poisoned.'

He unwraps the bandage. A crimson swollen gash across the palm.

'You cut yourself.'

'Alessandra is to blame!' He is almost shouting. 'The roof should have been repaired.'

'Alessandra isn't to blame that there was a storm-force gale in the summer. And she did tell you to put on her gardening gloves to handle the slates.'

'It was her fault.'

'Everything is always someone else's fault with you, isn't it?' her mother snaps.

'We won't go back.'

'Don't be ridiculous. You can't do that to Alessandra. She adores the child.'

The rocking of the train.

They think she has fallen asleep.

The sea did not sleep.

Billions upon billions of eggs – herring, cod, mackerel, haddock, whiting – release into the depths of the oceans; float amongst the multitude of plankton, secrete in the tentacles of jellyfish, dribble down to settle on the ocean floor . . .

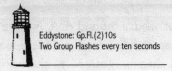

Chapter 14

'Not exactly your healthy breakfast' – Ben smiled at Saskia's raised eyebrows – 'but this dockside café caters for the men who've been out at sea.' He collected two plates heaped with fried potato scones, black pudding, sliced sausage and egg, and plonked them down on the table. 'Eat up,' he said. 'It's freezing out there.'

Despite the fact that they had arrived at Peterhead docks in what Saskia considered to be the middle of the night, the harbour area was already busy. As they left the café and walked in the direction of the quayside the sky was lightening to clearest blue and she could glimpse the open water beyond the harbour walls. Saskia felt the same uplift to her spirits she'd experienced when she had jumped down from the pick-up and walked to the cliff edge with Neil on the first day she arrived.

On an impulse she turned to Ben and said, 'Do you ever feel *different* when you are close by the sea? It's so hard to put into words. Sometimes I feel as if I'm in another space.'

Ben nodded in agreement. 'I think I know what you mean. If you're very busy you can forget to take the time

103

just to look at what's around you, but the sea won't be ignored.' He spread his arms to encompass the whole quayside and then he pointed to the horizon. 'You are drawn outwards and there is nothing between you and the sky. At times I watch the birds and wonder if they can appreciate their unique ability to defy gravity.'

'That's it,' said Saskia in excitement. 'It's almost like flying.'

Ben caught her gaze and smiled.

Saskia looked at him and saw how his eyes were dark and bright at the same time. Now don't get any ideas, she told herself severely. You can't cope with any more complications in your life at present.

'What I don't understand,' said Ben, 'is why you decided to do economics at university. It doesn't seem to suit you at all.'

'Well, I was very unsure, and my mum and dad – well, Dad really – thought it would be a good idea. You know how it is.'

'No,' said Ben.

Saskia looked away.

'Tell me,' said Ben, '. . . how it is.'

'Um . . .' How could she tell him? She didn't know herself.

As if he sensed her unease, he touched her lightly on the arm and kept chatting as they walked.

'They've only recently built a new fish market here. The old one couldn't cope with the volume of landings. Peterhead is the busiest white-fish port in Europe. Boats come and go all the time.' They stopped beside some boats where the men were loading empty fish boxes.

'These ones here have already landed their catch,' said Ben. 'The letters on the side are part of their registration details and let you know their home port . . . BCK is for Buckie, FR for Fraserburgh, NE, Newcastle, GY, Grimsby, and so on.'

Saskia read out the names painted on the bows. '*Star of Morning, Marie Hope, Sarah Ann, Frances Louise.* They have such lovely names,' she said.

'Fishermen often call their boat after their children or grandchildren. Female mostly,' Ben added.

If my grandfather had lived, thought Saskia, I might have had a boat named for me.

Saskia, Star of the Sea.

'The boats seem so small,' she said, 'to be out for days in all weathers.'

'They're pretty sturdy,' said Ben. 'Years ago the boats could only stand a Force Five gale, now they're out in a Force Eight. Conditions have improved, and so has safety, but it's still the most dangerous occupation there is.'

'Sounds terrifying. It's amazing that there are so many people still prepared to go to sea.'

'In a lot of British coastal towns and villages there's practically no other source of income. Fishing is the framework which supports the whole infrastructure of these communities. But apart from that, for many of them it's more than just a job. I think fishermen are born to it: in the heart and in the head. Even now, boys as young as ten or eleven want to go to sea with their dads. I know I did when I was that age.'

'Ahhh . . .' said Saskia. That explained a lot. 'You're from a fishing family?'

'My grandfather was a fisherman and so was my dad. But now my parents run a bed and breakfast in St Andrews. My father does some inshore fishing along the Fife coast, but my mother fears the sea. She calls it "the Widow-Maker". She's glad my job is land-based.'

They had walked as far as the long fish-market sheds. On the side facing the sea a few boats were tied up, unloading their catch. The men moved swiftly, winching the boxes full of fish up from the hold and swinging them across to the quayside. Here the boxes were stacked on little forklift trucks and then taken through one of the many doors that opened out all along the sheds. Ben and Saskia watched the men working for a few minutes before going inside.

'Slosh some disinfectant on the soles of your shoes,' said Ben, showing Saskia the trough just inside the door.

They stopped at the office to read the spreadsheet pinned up outside. Beside the name of each boat was a list of type of fish caught: MONKS, HADDOCK, DOGS, SHELLFISH.

'If the boats are supposed to catch only a certain type of fish,' said Saskia, 'how can they prevent other fish from swimming into their nets?'

'They can't,' said Ben. 'And the fish are very thrawn,' he laughed, 'because they stubbornly refuse to co-oper-ate with the Common Fisheries Policy by swimming together in the same species, in certain sizes, and in spec-ified numbers. Neil Buchan is right when he says the legislation is a mess. The decision-makers in Europe are blundering about and not getting it right on all counts. Their regulations cause endless problems for the fishermen, and as far as the scientists are concerned, the catch quotas set are above *their* ideal recommendations, so nobody is pleased. Fishermen have a big problem with the quotas. If it's the wrong type of fish, or their catch is over quota, what can they do? Throw the dead fish back into the sea? Many fishermen would consider that an offence against creation. And from a financial point of view it doesn't make sense. The fish are dead anyway: why not sell them anywhere you can?'

They arrived inside the market hall just as the auction began. Forklifts drove swiftly to and fro depositing more and more boxes full of fish piled with crushed ice. The huge shed was filling up rapidly with long lines of boxes, and buyers stepped among the boxes, examining the fish, and then gathered round the auctioneers as they moved through the shed.

Saskia and Ben walked into a rising surge of sound. The frantic gabble of the auctioneer and the buyers checking prices on their walkie-talkies battled against the shouts of market workers and the drag of the boxes on the concrete floor. Opposite the doors on the seaward side a row of metal shuttered doors opened onto the loading bays, where transport lorries were backed up. Every so often, with a roar of its engines, a lorry would leave its loading bay, growling away in the dawn to take the fish to the south and the continent of Europe. Some fishermen leaning against the wall watched their catch being sold. Saskia saw weariness in their posture, and thought the haggling almost disrespectful considering the effort required to bring in the fish.

'Why do they empty out some boxes?' asked Saskia,

looking at a pile of fish and crushed ice lying beside one upturned box.

'The buyers do it with an odd one or two,' said Ben. 'They're checking to make sure the box has been packed properly and that there are no smaller fish below covered up with the bigger, better fish.'

Saskia recalled the herring barrels in Alessandra's cellar with the marks scorched on the outside to show the contents.

Near a loading bay Ben spoke to one of the fishermen to ask if he had seen much seal activity. Saskia was only catching about one word in five, but could follow the conversation enough to know that the fisherman thought that the seal flu was spreading.

'Dead seals in the water,' she heard the man say. 'More than last week.'

'Denmark,' said another. 'It started ower there. Anholt Island.'

'There's a lot more seals dying than we thought at first,' said Ben. 'Trying to keep tabs on it is giving us a big headache.'

Saskia saw the buyers scattering little oblongs of paper in the boxes of sold fish and asked Ben what they were.

'They're markers with the buyers' names so that the men loading the lorries know where each consignment is going,' Ben explained.

The variety of the fish fascinated Saskia. It was the first time she had seen so many different species so close that she could touch them. She admired the colour, their sleek compacted bodies, their beauty, even in death.

'You know a Fraserburgh trawler caught a huge baby

giant squid not so long ago,' Ben told her. 'Half a mile down in Atlantic waters, a huge thing, nearly twice the size of you or me.'

'I'd love to see something like that,' said Saskia.

'It went to the National Marine Aquarium in Plymouth,' said Ben, 'but if you like looking at unusual species I can arrange for you to see round the Fhindhaven Marine Research Station if you're free sometime next week.'

'That would be great,' said Saskia. She hesitated before she spoke. 'I am due to go back to London at the end of next weekend.'

'What are you doing for the summer?' Ben asked as they left the shed and began to walk back to where his van was parked.

'This and that,' said Saskia. 'I kind of promised that I'd help my father with his business. His books have been in a mess since his accountant left.'

'Why?'

'Why what?'

'Why did your dad's accountant leave?'

'Oh . . .' Saskia hesitated. 'He emigrated or . . . something.'

They had almost reached the place where the van was parked.

'The reason I ask,' Ben went on, 'is that you might want to think about staying on here for the summer. The government has allocated extra funding to help out with the seal crisis and Fhindhaven Research Station could do with some assistance.'

This was the second time Ben had suggested that she

might stay on for the summer. Saskia glanced at his face. There was nothing there to indicate any special interest, no way for her to know if he cared personally whether she agreed or refused.

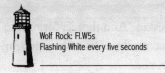
Chapter 15

The early start began to catch up with Saskia as Ben drove back to Fhindhaven from Peterhead. She didn't realize that her eyes had closed until Ben nudged her awake.

'Time to wake up, sleepyhead,' he said. 'We're almost there.'

Saskia sat up. They had reached the turn in the road where Neil had stopped the pick-up truck to let her see Cliff House. 'Oh, stop here, please,' she said. 'I'd like to look at this view.'

Ben pulled the van across the road. 'This was my first sight of my great-aunt's house,' said Saskia. 'Neil and I stopped to look down to the bay the day I arrived. Actually' – she turned to Ben – 'if you don't mind I'll just walk from here. I think I need some fresh air to wake me up.'

Ben leaned across and opened the van door. 'I'll speak to the education officer at Fhindhaven Marine Research Station at the beginning of next week and ask her when she can give you a tour. It'll probably be Wednesday afternoon, but I'll call you, shall I?'

'Fine,' said Saskia. 'And thanks for taking me to the fish market. I'm not really a morning person but that was worth the early rise.'

'Good.' Ben waited a second, as though he was going to say something else, but then only waved his hand and drove off.

Saskia watched the van disappear round the bend in the road. Was she disappointed he hadn't said anything more? If she had to be absolutely honest with herself, then yes, she probably was. Ben was more mature and confident than any of the boys she was friendly with at home, yet she was very much at ease with him. And then, there had been that moment at the harbour when he'd understood in an instant exactly what she had been thinking . . .

She looked at her watch. It was only just gone eleven o'clock. Alessandra was delivering material to the Heritage Centre this morning so she had given Saskia a front door key, but Saskia was in no hurry to return to Cliff House. From a chill dawn the day had brightened into a full spring morning and she wanted to take her time and enjoy it. Saskia wandered to the clifftop barrier. Beyond this was the section of the cliff that Neil had said was unsafe. Saskia realized that she was standing on the headland above the place where she had found the seal. Directly below would be the jagged rocks that her great-aunt thought dangerous. Now Saskia could understand why. Not far beyond the barrier the edge of the cliff had fallen away, exposing great chunks of crumbling earth and stones. It *was* dangerous. But despite this she was tempted to go nearer and so, with a quick jump, she climbed up and over the barrier, and walked a few steps towards the edge of the abyss.

Saskia drew in her breath. A child's picture-book illustration was spread before her: a sea of paint-box blue, little clouds feathered white across the sky, yellow sand scalloped with the creamy liqueur of curling waves. Immediately below her, massive jagged rocks guarded the headland. Around and between them the sea fretted, water sucking and churning in constant motion. The hypnotic swirling drew Saskia closer, hardly conscious that she had taken one or two more steps. She stopped. With an effort she pulled her eyes away.

Saskia retraced her steps and began to walk briskly down the right side of the road towards the house. It struck her that although man-made, the building was at one with the cliff, coming out from, yet seeming to be part of, the landscape. And it was not only she who saw the house as a part of its setting. Saskia recalled Ben, the first day they had met, being impressed with the house and the bay. She wondered if the cove had been used at one time for smuggling, and thought of the boats laden with fine silks and barrels of brandy coming round past those dangerous reefs and beaching on the shingle.

Saskia was almost at the point where the house would be hidden again by the turn of the road when her gaze caught the briefest of movements at one of the attic windows. Alessandra must have returned from the Heritage Centre. Perhaps she had gone into the attic to check it was safe, as she had promised Saskia she would. Saskia hurried down the road to the house. She was eager to see what childhood 'treasures' of hers were still up there.

Twenty stairs to the top floor. Saskia turned the handle. The door was unlocked. She stepped inside.

There was no one there.

Beside the door were piles and piles of old fishing nets, heaped up almost to the low roof. Here and there lay other fishing gear, lobster creels, floats, a pile of blankets, one or two barrels, and some old shoe boxes filled with shells. Apart from these things the attic was empty.

Saskia moved further into the room. A few thin tatters of old lace hung down on each side of the windows. Saskia fingered the remnants and felt the wind blow through the gap in the window frames. The movement she had seen from the road must have been these old curtains flapping in the breeze.

There was a noise behind her. Saskia jumped. Someone was on the outside stairs. Silently the door handle began to turn. Saskia fixed her eyes on the door.

The door opened slowly and her great-aunt stepped into the room.

'Saskia!' Alessandra cried.

Saskia rocked back a little on her feet.

'Are you all right?'

Saskia nodded, suddenly aware that she had been slightly frightened.

'I did ask you not to come up here,' said Alessandra. 'Parts of the roof aren't safe.'

'I was walking back along the coast road and I thought I saw you at the attic window. But it was just the net curtain flapping. This window frame is quite rotted and there's a draught coming through.'

Alessandra looked around her. 'I don't come up here very often.' She stepped back out of the room.

Saskia followed her and they walked together down the outside stairs and into the house.

Alessandra put her shopping bags on the kitchen table. With forced cheerfulness she said, 'Let's eat dinner by the fire in the big room tonight. We might play some more of the interview tapes.'

'Yes,' said Saskia. She suddenly felt enormously tired. Too early a start to the day, she told herself, tension within Alessandra, and – she was sure – some unresolved issue to do with her visits to Cliff House in the past. By next week her mother would surely be home and then she could talk to her, and ask her about her childhood summers here.

In the early evening Saskia and Alessandra prepared their meal together. The routine of peeling potatoes and chopping vegetables seemed to steady her great-aunt and, Saskia realized, had helped her regain her own equilibrium.

She'd slept in the afternoon and on wakening had lain for a while on her bed listening and thinking. The sea outside her window was soothing. Even the urgent cries of the nesting birds were not intrusive, being as they were intrinsic to her surroundings. The house too was settled. But – Saskia propped herself up on her pillows – was there within it, within *her*, a restlessness? The building *did* shift and susurrate, as Alessandra said it did. This afternoon easing itself, from time to time, into the cliff, or . . .

Saskia's eyes blinked wide open. Did it mirror the

mood of its occupants? Certainly she was calmer than she had been earlier. And she knew Alessandra was sitting quietly by the kitchen door splitting wood for kindling. When she thought back on the last few days Saskia could see that, to begin with, she had been on edge, nervous of living with a person known as slightly peculiar, wrong-footed from the beginning with her incomplete memories of former visits. But now she was becoming accustomed to the atmosphere of this place. Saskia got up and went over and patted the wall of her bedroom that rested against the cliff . . . and felt strangely better for having done it.

And being thus so much more relaxed, as she and Alessandra sat that night, plates on knees, eating in front of the fire, instead of agreeing to listen to the interview tapes Saskia said, 'Actually, I'd rather hear *your* memories, Alessandra. From when you were about my age. You told me that you packed herring in barrels. I noticed this morning that the fish in the market at Peterhead were sorted in boxes before they came off the boat.'

'I only went the twice,' said Alessandra. 'And it was after the Second World War, so the great days of the herring fishing were passing even then.'

'What happened during the war?' asked Saskia.

'Most of the men went away. To the Royal Navy or the Merchant Navy. We are an island. We needed the Atlantic convoys or we would have starved. A lot of fishermen did mine-sweeping duties. Many did not return. One in four of the merchant fleet lost their lives.'

'Ben says that, even outside wartime, sea fishing is reckoned to be the most dangerous profession,' said Saskia.

'Aye, we work hard to win our living from the sea.'

'And after the war?' Saskia prompted.

'After the war, Fraserburgh was the chief herring town in Scotland. The boats and the fishing methods were changing but men still hunted the herring. The shoals moved round the British Isles in what the old ones said was a magic circle. As we lived from one year's end to another, so it was with the herring, passing as the seasons did. Winter fishing began early in the year, mainly up in the far north and the Western Isles. From May to September we had the summer fishing. It started in the Shetland Isles, and as the fish swam south, so the fishing fleet followed the shoals: Fraserburgh, Peterhead, Aberdeen, the Tyne ports, Grimsby, Yarmouth, Lowestoft.'

'I know it was hard work,' said Saskia, 'but it must have been a change of routine to see different places.'

'And the old photographs and film don't show ye the colour,' said Alessandra. 'The boats were awfu' braw, funnels and wheelhouses painted bright colours, red and dark blues and greens, lettering picked out in gold or yellow. When they came by into the harbour it was a sicht tae see. Mak' ye proud to be a herring quine.'

Alessandra looked into the fire. Saskia saw that she was smiling.

'The boats would come in where their own lassies were working. We went down on the train mostly, although some girls travelled by boat. I was just sixteen the first time I went, and very excited to be away from home and going to a different place. Yarmouth was one of the better ports: there were lodging houses rather than huts to stay in.'

'Huts?' said Saskia. 'That doesn't sound very comfortable.'

Alessandra almost laughed at this. 'Comfort was not a consideration.' She gestured at their empty plates lying beside the hearth. 'For most of us the major concern was having a full stomach through the winter.'

Saskia stretched out in her chair and rested her feet on the fender. On the other side of the fireplace her great-aunt did the same. We are at each end of an arc between three generations, Saskia thought. She recalled herself allowing Ben to throw away her can of juice despite the fact that there was some left in it. From hunger to waste in less than a lifetime.

'Each girl brought a kist of belongings.' Alessandra glanced at Saskia. 'You know the word "kist"? It means a chest. A chest full of things to see you through the season – clothes, and hairbrush and comb and such like. We needed heavy clothes to keep us warm, and stout boots too. The girls wore different shawls depending on which village they came from: Inverallochy and Cairnbulg had black and red checks, St Combs and Fhindhaven, black and blue. We wore long oilskin aprons. By the end of a day they were covered in fish guts and blood. The rules were strict and it was a twelve-hour shift, longer if more boats came in, but for me it was a blessed freedom. An' we had a' Sunday to dress up and walk out. Ye'd link arms as ye walked about the town and the sea front, and all the lads would stand to watch ye stroll by, and call out as ye passed, but ye jist gave them no mind . . . or at least ye didn't let on ye heard them.'

Alessandra broke off and looked across the room at

Saskia. 'Ben,' she said, 'that young man you went into Peterhead with this morning. Do you like him?'

'Alessandra!' exclaimed Saskia. 'What a question.'

'Aye. So ye do then.' Alessandra smiled at her.

'Let's go back to you gutting fish,' said Saskia, but she too was smiling.

'I was a packer. It saved my hands. I would bind Chris and May's fingers each morning with strips of cloth cut from old flour bags, and tie them up with thread to try to protect them from being slashed or nicked by the knife. The knives were sharp, very sharp. If a cut turned septic ye'd be sent home.' Alessandra looked down at her hands, at the once strong brown fingers. 'It's hard to believe the speed at which the girls worked. We stood by the farlins, big open troughs, and they brought the herring there straight from the boat and emptied them in. They were gutted and graded in seconds, and I packed the barrels. One layer, tails this way, the next layer, tails that way, and so on. And the salt o' course between them a'. Seven hundred fish in less than ten minutes. The barrels were left for nigh a fortnight to let the fish settle and the ullage topped up each morning with more fish. Then a Fishery Board inspector sealed and branded them.'

'Did each barrel need to be passed by the Fishery Board?' asked Saskia. 'In Peterhead this morning the buyers tipped out boxes to inspect the fish underneath.'

'It wasn't compulsory, but a branded barrel sold for more than an unbranded one.'

'Were the fish graded by size?' asked Saskia, thinking again of the boxes in Peterhead fish market.

'Their quality was set according to their own life cycle,' said Alessandra. 'See, forbye them moving through the sea with the months of the year, the fish had their own season within the shoal, and ye named them and graded them for that. *Matties* were maiden fish, fat before the roe was grown in them. *Fulls* were full of fish roe and ready to spawn. And *Spent* were the ones whose time of spawning had passed, and they were valued the least.

'Now as I think on it, it seems to reflect our journey through life.' She smiled at Saskia. 'But it is time you had a happy story from this house, and I was happy then, very happy. We were a' young and full o' life and had no time to dwell on things. So many people. All around the quays, with the boats and the fishermen, and the curers and the carters, and children running between, and the talk of the girls, and the cry of the gulls, and the sweet, sweet smell of freedom.'

Alessandra smiled. 'I can hardly go tae any harbour and see and smell the boats, an' the fish, an' not think on it. There was a rhythm in it all. The rhythm of life itself.'

Chapter 16

In the arctic seas huge jellyfish, two metres across, feared by fishermen for tearing nets and stinging the skin, shelter the cod fry between their poisonous tentacles. Drifting with the tides they carry the baby cod, protecting them for the crucial first days of life, away from their predators to the safer inshore waters.

'Investigation into fish and fishing has been going on for a very long time,' said Ben. 'Probably since Stone Age man stood, spear in hand, by the edge of a stretch of water trying to catch fish.'

He was standing with Saskia looking at the display in the reception area of the Fhindhaven Marine Research Station, waiting for the education officer to join them. He placed his finger on the map of the British Isles to where the northeast shoulder of Scotland thrust out into the sea.

'Do you know that Kinnaird Head appears on a map plotted by Ptolemy over two thousand years ago?'

Saskia moved closer to see the point of land near Fraserburgh. She was aware of Ben's breath on her cheek.

Ben turned his head. He looked into her face. 'You have extraordinary coloured hair,' he said.

Saskia stepped back. 'I think the sun here has lightened it.'

'Mmmm.' Ben nodded, not taking his eyes from hers. 'It suits you.'

Saskia held his gaze and felt herself smile. 'Thank you.'

He nodded again, and then glanced over her shoulder. 'Here comes Ailsa.' He raised his voice. 'Our *wonderful* education officer. I've asked her to give you a guided tour.'

'Watch it, you.' Ailsa smiled at him. 'Careful of this one,' she said to Saskia. 'He's forever trying to get people to work extra-long hours.'

Ben grinned. 'Always in a good cause, though.'

'I'll grant you that,' said Ailsa. 'It usually is something worthwhile.'

'I'll leave you with Ailsa.' Ben touched Saskia on the arm. 'Catch you later.'

'I expect Ben's been showing you the display boards,' said Ailsa, 'so I won't go over that part of the introduction again.'

'What?' Saskia turned her attention to Ailsa. 'Sorry, yes, we did have a quick look at them.'

'Well, you can read them later in as much detail as you want, but from earliest times humans have been interested in marine life, mainly as a source of food. If you look at items recovered from ancient historical sites then you can see that our ancestors must have put a certain amount of thought into designing something even as basic as the fishing hook. Now in order to do that, it's obvious that someone studied a few different aspects of marine life. Nowadays we still see the sea as a resource to be used – for food, oil, gas, minerals – but recently there has been a greater urgency to balance the environment. We know that we have to preserve and conserve or we will jeopardize the future.'

'Do you think we are almost at crisis level?' Saskia asked as she followed Ailsa on her tour through the various aquariums and labs.

'Yes,' Ailsa replied seriously. 'But it's a hard fact for people to face. For a start it isn't obvious, except to those involved in scientific research, and then there is the very real issue that, for the peoples of some nations, it's a choice between survival and conservation.'

'I think Ben takes it very seriously,' said Saskia.

'Ben is incredibly dedicated and cares deeply about his work,' replied Ailsa.

Saskia recalled Ben's conversation with Neil in Alessandra's kitchen. What she had taken for arrogance in Ben had in fact been someone speaking confidently about a subject he knew.

'The North Sea itself is quite shallow, but there is a deeper stretch of water going into the Atlantic known as the Faroe Shetland Channel. A huge amount of extensive research is planned for that area in the future. Ben is working with our hydrologists who are studying ocean currents. We're devising programmes of simulation to track how nutrients are distributed. Water movements of enormous depth and distance bring phytoplankton to the surface for zoo plankton to feed on. The fluctuations of the plankton are crucial to the planet. Larger sea creatures

123

feed on smaller ones, big fish eat little fish, and many fish rely on the plankton. Colonies of sea birds all over the world do too, and so does,' she added with a dry laugh, 'the greediest predator and major polluter of the planet – us.'

In one of the labs Ailsa had set up some specimens for Saskia to inspect. Saskia looked through the microscope at the tiny sea organisms, some less than a millimetre in length. Could the future of the planet depend on something so minute?

'We've had ocean research vessels going out from the Northeast for over one hundred years.' Ailsa showed Saskia the library and archive files. 'I spend the odd afternoon browsing through the older research papers here. I find it amazing the amount of detail collected in ships that had so much less high-tech equipment than we have now.'

Ailsa led Saskia from the library to the staff room, talking as she went.

'An official Fishery Board was established in Scotland in the eighteen eighties with a remit "to improve and regulate the fisheries", but there are many other organizations involved in marine research. Ben has probably told you about the Gatty Laboratory at St Andrews University where he studied. There are others located around the British Isles and Northern Ireland, and we have contacts with similar types of research world wide. Are you interested in marine studies?'

'I don't know . . .' Saskia hesitated.

'The subject is so wide-ranging. From studying tissues in labs to trips on our research ships. The Arctic is a favourite of mine – the colours within the ice are spectacular. But I don't think it's a good idea to decide to live anywhere until you've spent a year or two in the place.' Ailsa smiled. 'Some winter days, up here, it's dark at half past three.'

'And the summers?'

'The summers can be beautiful, though there aren't as many really hot days as you would get further south, but' – Ailsa smiled – 'the sky is light until after midnight.'

'I saw the aurora borealis the first night I arrived,' said Saskia.

'That would be last week, wouldn't it? One of the girls who works here said she had seen them. She lives on a farm. I think they are more noticeable if you are away from street lighting.'

'I've never seen anything like it,' said Saskia. 'It was stunning.'

'At the risk of sounding boring, I think natural wonders of the world outclass anything man-made.' Ailsa handed Saskia a mug of coffee. 'Have you thought about taking up marine studies in any structured way?'

'Not really.' Saskia leaned back into her chair. 'When I was little I loved being near the sea, but my parents' attitude was that it was a childish thing that you grew out of. My father especially was always very uneasy about my fascination with it. He came from a fishing family where there was a lot of tragedy. And as I got older I did as he suggested because I wanted to please him . . .' Saskia stopped. 'It sounds pretty stupid, doesn't it?'

'Not at all.' Ailsa picked up her own coffee and made a face into the mug. 'I can empathize with that. I was exactly the same. My father was a marine biologist and I wanted to go into teaching. So to please him I did one of the marine-based courses at Aberdeen University and then teacher training afterwards. I find this job very fulfilling, but it took me *years* before I was doing what I wanted.'

'At home it was always sort of understood that I'd eventually go into my father's property business,' said Saskia. 'I *think* I'd like this type of work, but I'm not sure if I'm attracted to the work itself, or being near the sea, or—'

She had nearly mentioned Ben's name and Saskia felt her face go a bit pink, but Ailsa seemed not to have noticed.

'Well, taking a summer placement is certainly the way to get an insight without committing yourself.'

Saskia sipped her coffee. Her mind was now a mixture of confusing thoughts. She had to be sure that she was taking the job because *she* wanted to. Not because she was attracted to Ben, or even because of the lab's physical location close to the sea.

Ailsa put her head on one side and looked at Saskia. 'If you do decide to stay here for the summer, what will your parents and your great-aunt think about it?'

Instinctively, Saskia knew that her great-aunt would be happy to hear her news, and felt a little glow of pleasure at Alessandra's reaction when she told her.

Alessandra's face coloured and her eyes smiled out in the briefest flash, then she masked them again. 'You must do what you want to do, Saskia. But you are most welcome to stay here.'

'I don't have to,' said Saskia. 'The Research Station said they could probably find me cheap accommodation.'

'I'd be glad if you stayed here.'

'I would be able to contribute to my keep,' said Saskia.

'Oh, child!' Alessandra let out a little cry. 'That is not an issue. You eat like a sparrow and anyway, I am not so poor that I cannot share bread with you.'

Her father's reaction left Saskia shaken and confused.

'What kind of work is this? You can easily find a job in London where you don't need to be away from home.'

'I thought you'd be pleased. I'll be spending more time with Aunt Alessandra,' Saskia said in a small voice. She hated any disagreement with her father and sensed a major row looming.

'I don't want you getting any strange ideas. I thought I'd managed to get all that sea nonsense out of your head years ago.'

Saskia held the receiver away from her for a moment. *Nonsense?* she mouthed in the air . . . Nonsense!

'It's not *nonsense*, Dad,' she protested. 'It's valuable work. You remember I found that sick seal on the beach. Well, they think a virus is attacking the seal population. If it becomes an epidemic they'll need a bit of support.'

'A few seals dying off isn't a major concern, surely. You've got more important things to do.'

'Like what?'

'Like doing what you're supposed to be doing,' her father snapped. 'Talking up Alessandra to invest in my property development. I don't think you realize how important this is to me.'

127

To you.

'Who have you been listening to anyway that's got you thinking about doing this? Alessandra would never have made this suggestion. Someone must have put the idea your head.'

'I *am* capable of having an idea of my own, Dad,' Saskia said stiffly.

'No you're not.'

Saskia gasped.

'You're not, Saskia,' her father insisted. 'You're not able to make a decision like this. You never have before.'

'I can. I have. I decided on my trip to Nepal.'

'Don't be silly. It was *me* who did that.'

Saskia's stomach fell away. For a moment or two she couldn't speak. 'What do you mean, *you* decided on the trip to Nepal?'

'Of course it was me. I got the maps, didn't I? I looked up the information.'

Saskia gripped the receiver. Her father *had* bought books and magazines that featured Nepal, cut articles from newspapers, spotted adverts for treks around Katmandu.

Why?

'Why?' Saskia put her thoughts into speech. 'Why did you want me to go to Nepal?'

'It looked like an interesting place.'

But now Saskia knew there was more. He did not take so much time and trouble over something without there being another reason.

'Why?' she shouted into the receiver. 'Why Nepal?'

128

'You were talking about Australia. Some crazy idea about swimming off the Great Barrier Reef—'

Understanding came to Saskia before he had finished the sentence.

Nepal is landlocked.

'You knew that I was determined to go off somewhere but you didn't want me near an ocean for weeks on end.' Her voice shook. 'Why not?'

He tried charm. 'You know I have only your best interests at heart, Saskia,' he said.

'You have an emotional hang-up about the sea,' she said bitterly, and didn't care that she was repeating one of her mother's phrases.

'Don't be impertinent.'

'It wasn't meant to be.'

There was a silence. 'Yes,' her father said finally, 'I do have concerns about any career for you connected with the sea. And with my family history it's understandable. But apart from that, it's more sensible for you to come into the business with me, so I really need to keep you on target.'

'What about what *I* want?' said Saskia.

'But this *is* what you want,' he said. 'You always said that you'd come into the business with me.'

'No, I didn't. *You* said it.'

'But you never said otherwise.'

'I tried to. You don't listen.'

'Come on, Saskia,' he wheedled. 'Be fair. You murmured a few protests from time to time, but you never fundamentally disagreed.'

He was right. She hadn't. For the most part they got

on well together and he had told her how much fun it would be to go abroad on property-buying trips. She felt herself waver. Simpler to go home at the end of this week and get on with the rest of her life. Through the window of the call box she could see the boats in the harbour. There were tears gathering behind her eyelids.

'Saskia?'

She pushed the door open a little with her foot to get some air. Through the noise of the gulls she heard a boat engine turn over.

'I'm taking this job for the summer.'

She heard her father's sharp intake of breath. Then he said, 'I won't be able to send you money.'

Saskia stared at the phone mouthpiece. He had done this before. If he did not approve of her actions, he withheld financial support; but more importantly – Saskia experienced a moment of clarity – emotional support.

He withheld his love.

There was a cobweb in the call box. In a corner of the roof silvery filaments spread in a complex concentric pattern. A work of technical engineering brilliance, beautiful to behold. She saw the insect trapped there, a fly, one wing fluttering, still alive and, Saskia knew, it would still be alive when the spider decided to cocoon it. Did it feel comforted to begin with, she wondered, as it was wrapped round with the delicate silken thread? To be swaddled against the world *was* comforting. It relieved you of the need to make decisions. And it would be so much easier not to hold out against him. For she knew her father's behaviour pattern. Any moment now would come the blistering rage, one of the terrifying and dangerous outbursts that she dreaded, that she'd do anything to avoid.

She heard herself say, 'Actually, Dad, I'll be nowhere near the sea. It's mainly indoor filing of records, paperwork mostly.'

'Oh. I didn't realize that.'

'Yes,' she prattled on. 'Great-aunt Alessandra says I can stay on with her for a bit. I'll be able to get to know her better and that will fit in with whatever you've got planned.'

So now she had become a deceiver. She had lied to her father – well, perhaps not quite lied, but moved the truth sideways.

It was what he did.

All the time.

He had told Alessandra that she, Saskia, desperately wanted to visit her, which wasn't true. He had passed off as his idea the suggestion that she should bring her bike, when it had been Alessandra's idea. Her father tampered with the truth to get what he wanted.

Now she had done the same.

Chapter 17

Alessandra put down the book she had been reading.

'I do not know how to answer your question truth-fully, Saskia. There may be more than one reason why your parents stopped visiting me. Your father once told me that you yourself had said that you did not want to come back here, that you had been so frightened by the storm you were terrified to return and he did not want to force you. But it was not a complete puzzlement to me that your father did not come back to visit me after the summer of nineteen seventy-six.' Alessandra lifted her head and looked directly at Saskia. 'Your memory in your dream was correct. Your father was angry with me.'

'About the roof?' said Saskia. 'I know that he likes his own way but it does seem a bit extreme that he would not visit you again because you argued about repairing the roof.'

'Not just the roof. That was the catalyst to spark his anger.'

'What then?' And as Alessandra did not reply, Saskia went on, 'It's really very important for me that you tell

132

me, Alessandra. I am almost an adult. I know my father has faults and perhaps you don't like to discuss them with me. But this is something that I need to sort out.'

'He was angry with me,' Alessandra began hesitantly, 'because I would not invest more money in his business. I had done so in the past and he automatically expected me to do so again. But I had not enough money, although I don't think he believed me.'

'So he did not come back to visit you because you would not lend him more money? How horrible!' cried Saskia.

'No, I don't think that was the whole reason,' said Alessandra. 'He said that *you* insisted that they never came back.'

Saskia was angry. 'He avoids truth,' she said. 'You must know that if you know him at all.'

Alessandra shook her head. 'Maybe so, but your mother also said this quite emphatically. I'm sure that she would have returned and brought you with her. She enjoyed her holidays here. You and I played together every day and it gave her time to paint. Your mother said that it was she you told, not your father, that they must never return.'

Alessandra's face had such a look of regret that Saskia wanted to cry. 'I'm so sorry,' she whispered. 'I have no idea why I said that. I am so sorry.'

At the end of the week Saskia's mother phoned her.

'I've just got back from my painting trip and your father tells me that you have decided to stay in Scotland for the summer?'

Saskia closed her mind to her mother's implied accusation of desertion. 'Yes,' she said.

'I don't know if I'll be able to come up and join you at all.'

'I think I might manage on my own.'

'Really?' Her mother's voice sharper now. 'You know you took a big dislike to that place when you were a child.'

'Actually, Mum, I wanted to ask you about that. Dad and Great-aunt Alessandra say that when I was six years old I told you I never wanted to come back.'

'That's right. You did.'

'Did I say why?'

'Not specifically. Something scared you so much that you said you didn't want ever to go back there.'

'What?' said Saskia. 'What could it have been?'

'I don't know. The last year we were there a freak gale nearly took the whole roof off.'

'My memory is that I thought the storm was very exciting. Why would I say that I did not want to return?'

'Maybe you just grew out of that kind of holiday. At that age Disney would be much more attractive.'

'I don't think that was the reason, Mum. There's something else that I just can't quite remember. When I said I didn't want to come back, why did you and Dad listen to me anyway?'

'Because, darling, you were terrified. I don't know why. You made me promise never to speak of it. It was when you were ill.'

'When I was ill?'

'You had screaming nightmares. It was awful. You were sleepwalking all over the house.'

'I was sleepwalking?'

'Yes. We thought you were having some kind of break-down.'

'Tell me more about it,' said Saskia.

Her mother paused. 'Your illness was a great strain for your father and me, you know.'

'I do know,' Saskia said coldly. 'You have told me *many* times.'

'Really, Saskia. I dislike your tone. A child never knows what sacrifices a parent has made to bring them up.'

Well this one does, thought Saskia, because she has been reminded often enough. Instead she spoke firmly. 'Yes, but I was a *child*, with a limited reasoning and power, and it was not *my* responsibility to bring *me* up. Dad and you were, are, the adults, and in any case,' she added quickly, 'I don't want to get bogged down in that old, old story. I want to know why it suddenly happened that we did not return here, to Cliff House? What happened to me?'

There was silence.

'Tell me.'

'All I know,' her mother spoke tersely, 'is that we never came back after you caught meningitis.'

Meningitis!

That was the word she had heard whispered in the night when she had been ill. The name of her illness. She had been too young to understand, too young to remember clearly.

'You were close to death. I think your father blamed Alessandra. He said her water supply was not fresh or there were pollutants on the beach.'

135

'What year was that?'

'Nineteen seventy-seven.'

Saskia replaced the receiver. She had a lot to think about. She took a piece of paper and wrote out the years. This was 1988. From her great-aunt's photograph albums she knew that she had last visited Cliff House in the summer of 1976. She had been six years old. And she had been taken ill in 1976 – but it had been the *winter* of 1976, November and December. In the bookcase, beside books on fish and shells, she found a medical dictionary. Saskia looked up meningitis.

The information was clear. There was no way she had been exposed to meningitis at her great-aunt's house. Her last visit to Alessandra's house had been in the summer of 1976 and she had not become ill until November 1976. But that did not explain why she herself had not wanted to come back. Her mother had said that it was she, Saskia, who had insisted they should not return.

Little threads of recollection trailed loose, and she shuttled across the loom of her memory trying to weave them together.

It came to her that she had been frightened, very frightened, all through the autumn of 1976, but . . . that meant she had been frightened *before* she had caught meningitis. It hadn't been the illness that frightened her. She had been too young to know how seriously ill she was, only aware of being in hospital, that there were doctors and nurses around her. One nurse . . . in the night, by her bed in the hospital, a woman standing consoling her mother, saying, This is not the worst case we've seen in this outbreak. *In this outbreak.* She could check the local newspaper files when she got home but Saskia knew now that there must have been several cases of meningitis in their area when she was young. That was proof that her illness had nothing to do with Alessandra or Alessandra's house.

But her father, with his own fear of the sea and having had a huge row with Alessandra, was probably secretly pleased that Saskia had said she did not want to return to Cliff House. And he had not really *needed* her great-aunt's money at that time. His business was able to cope without Alessandra's investment.

But now . . .

Of course! Saskia's mind filled with the lines of the business accounts book. In particular the book he had snatched out of her hand. He dealt with ingoings, he told her. But there were no ingoings. His income had dwindled to nothing over the last few years and he was too proud to tell anyone about it. She should have picked up the signs before this. He had sold her pony when she was in Nepal, and their holiday cottage in the Lake District had gone the year before last. It had been the source of a major row with her mother, who went there to paint any time Saskia was away from home. He must be running short of money. That's why he had let his accountant go. Her father's story about his accountant emigrating was just a device to avoid the truth.

When she had first looked over her father's books, Saskia had phoned the accountant for information and, during the course of the conversation, had asked him when he was moving to America. He'd said that he wasn't going anywhere at the moment. When she had asked her father about this, he had replied quickly, 'Oh, maybe I got that wrong. His wife is having a baby, I think, and *then* they're going to Canada, land of opportunity – wish it were me. Don't worry about it anyway. I'll get a new accountant soon.'

A few weeks later she had met the accountant by chance and asked if they'd had their baby, and when they were leaving for Canada.

'Is that what your father told you?' he said, and smiled.

A slow insinuation began to insert itself into Saskia's mind. Her father's business was in much more trouble than he was prepared to admit. He'd told her that he wanted her to make friends with Alessandra again so that Alessandra would invest in his new project. But he wasn't thinking of how much profit Alessandra would make. Alessandra's money must be essential to this business venture. He wanted to ask his aunt for money but could not do it while they were still estranged. And her mother knew or suspected this was the reason he'd encouraged Saskia to travel north. When they had talked about it, Saskia now remembered her mother looking across at her father and saying, 'Not *us. You.*' Her mother knew that he had some scheme in his head even if she did not know what it was exactly. Her father's business crisis was why he had engineered her visit to her great-aunt Alessandra.

And, Saskia saw, none of what her father had said was a complete lie, but at the same time it was not quite the whole truth.

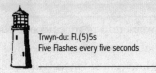

Chapter 18

Towards the end of the second week of Saskia's visit she and Alessandra went out together on their bikes. They took one of the coastal pathways and stopped to photograph a huddle of ruined cottages above a stretch of beach. Apart from a man walking his dog there was no one else in sight for miles. Alessandra's manner was becoming more relaxed in Saskia's company and they worked well together, photographing and writing up the information on the fishing villages. This part of Alessandra's heritage project was almost finished, and Saskia had made arrangements with the Marine Research Station to begin work there on Monday.

As they cycled home Saskia's mind was caught up with different thoughts. Ben had phoned. They had arranged to see a film in Aberdeen together at the weekend. So he must be interested in her not just as a volunteer for the seal crisis. Unless – she smiled to herself – the film turned out to be one about whales rather than the thriller he'd suggested. Even if the movie was about marine life their outing could still be looked on as a proper date. Saskia was already sorting out in her head what she might wear and regretting only having packed very casual clothes.

Saskia was cycling a little ahead and was first to reach the top of the road at Cliff House. She dismounted and turned round to watch her great-aunt, who was cycling more slowly as the road became steeper. Alessandra looked up and saw Saskia. She raised her hand to wave, and as she did so her bike began to wobble. In the next instant, Alessandra lost control and the front wheel twisted inwards. She was propelled across the handlebars and both she and the bike crashed down into the ditch at the side of the road.

Saskia threw her own bike aside and ran back down the hill. When she saw the way her great-aunt's body was twisted under the bike Saskia's heart gave a jump of fear.

'I'm going to phone for an ambulance,' she cried. Alessandra was conscious but moaning in pain. 'Don't try to move,' Saskia added. 'I'll be back soon.'

The ambulance came from the local cottage hospital and within half an hour Alessandra was being examined by the doctor on duty there.

Saskia sat in the waiting area until a nurse came and called her through. 'The doctor has just told Miss Granton that it looks like a bad ankle break. We're waiting for a radiographer. It will be a few hours at least before we've checked everything out.' She looked at Saskia. 'We'll admit your great-aunt to a ward so that she can have a rest. You might want to go home and get something to eat and come back later.'

Saskia took in how pale and nervous Alessandra appeared. 'I'd rather not leave my aunt on her own.'

'It's all right,' said Alessandra. 'This will take hours. I'll probably sleep for a little while and I would be happier if you went home and rested too.'

On her way out of the Casualty Department, the nurse who had admitted Alessandra to hospital spoke to Saskia. 'When you come back this evening, would you bring some night things for Miss Granton, please?'

'I didn't know that she would have to stay in,' said Saskia.

'She might not have to, but . . . just in case she does.'

At the bus stop opposite the hospital Saskia caught the Aberdeen bus, which went through Fhindhaven, and the driver dropped her at the pathway leading to Cliff House. She put her own bike away and then went back to the ditch where her great-aunt's bike still lay. The wheel was badly buckled and she had to hoist it onto her shoulder and carry it to the cellar. It gave her a strange feeling to look at it.

After she'd eaten she phoned Neil Buchan to tell him of Alessandra's accident. With Fhindhaven being such a small town, and as Neil was the taxi driver, Saskia thought he might know already. He didn't, and she was surprised at how upset he sounded on hearing the news.

'This is not good,' he said, 'not good at all.'

'Hopefully it's only a broken ankle,' said Saskia.

'Still it's not good,' said Neil. 'She'll go crazy if they try to keep her in.'

'Well, I'll find out more when I go back later today,' said Saskia. 'They said they might want her to remain there overnight so I've got a few things to look out for her.'

'You're all right being in the house by yourself?'

'Well, yes,' said Saskia.

'She'll hate it if she has to remain in the hospital for any length of time,' said Neil. 'Be warned.'

'Warned about what?' Saskia laughed.

'If they keep her in, she'll . . . she . . .' He paused. 'It frightens her.'

'What frightens her?' asked Saskia.

'Being away from the house.'

Saskia began to gather up some night things for Alessandra. She collected various toiletries from the downstairs bathroom that her great-aunt used and then crossed the hall into Alessandra's bedroom. There were no curtains or blinds in this room. The sea filled Saskia's eyes and ears and mind. A huge double-fronted window from ceiling almost to the floor looked straight out towards the east, where the sun rose each morning. Some drawings and sketches and colour washes lay stacked against one wall. They seemed faintly familiar, and then in surprise Saskia saw that her mother's signature was on them. Apart from that the room was frugally furnished. A great triple wardrobe took up the space along one wall. It was locked. A key was in the lock of the single door. Saskia hesitated. Perhaps she would find what she needed without having to unlock anything. She went to the old-fashioned dressing table, with its central mirror and column of drawers on either side. There was nothing on it, no photograph or perfume bottle, no comb or hairbrush. She thought of the clutter of her own room at home, her styling gel, hair spray; her mother's elaborate array of night creams and nail varnishes. Feeling slightly like a thief Saskia pulled out a drawer or two and found underwear, socks and a nightdress. Finally she took a dressing gown from the back of the door and set out for the hospital.

Chapter 19

When Saskia reached the hospital she was directed to the ward where Alessandra was resting. The sister there took her aside.

'Before you speak to your great-aunt I think you should know that she became a bit agitated when we told her that she might have to stay in for a couple of days. She's been asking for you.'

'I thought you said it was only to be overnight,' said Saskia.

The ward sister smiled easily. 'Her ankle is broken and she shouldn't really put any weight on it at all for a few days. We'll take good care of her.'

Alessandra was sitting up in bed, the whiteness of the hospital nightgown throwing the lines of her face into high relief.

'I must go home. I cannot stay here.'

'But you need to have your ankle seen to and everything else checked out,' Saskia said.

Alessandra shook her head.

Saskia gave her great-aunt an encouraging smile. 'It's only for a couple of days. They'll keep you in for observation and then discharge you.'

Alessandra twisted her fingers tightly together. Her voice was barely above a whisper. 'I don't want to stay here, Saskia.'

Saskia leaned closer. 'Alessandra, your ankle is broken,' she said gently. 'The nurses seem very nice. They'll take care of you.'

Alessandra glanced around her. 'I have to be careful.'

'Why?'

'They might take me . . . away.'

'Who?' asked Saskia, and as her great-aunt did not answer, she persisted: 'Who might take you away? Why would anyone want to do that?'

Now Alessandra's eyes were darting here and there. She looked around the ward as if searching for someone.

'No one can force you to go somewhere you don't want to go,' said Saskia.

Alessandra laughed, a shrill sound. 'They can. I told you. For a while I wasn't well . . . After my father . . . and all the rest . . . died. I wasn't well. Mentally. '

'That might have happened in the past,' said Saskia, 'but it won't happen now.'

Alessandra turned her head away sharply.

'It's quite normal to be like that after someone close to you has died. But there's nothing wrong with your mind now,' said Saskia. 'You get upset easily, but surely you don't need to be hospitalized.'

Alessandra shook her head again. And then Saskia realized that the movement was not voluntary. Her great-aunt was in the grip of some kind of nervous twitch. Her head jerked from side to side.

'Please calm down,' said Saskia in alarm.

She took the water glass and held it to her great-aunt's lips. Alessandra's body shook with a continuous tremor and water slopped over her chin.

A nurse hurried over. 'The doctor prescribed some sedatives earlier. I'll ask the ward sister if she can take them now.' She came back a few moments later with some tablets which she managed to get Alessandra to swallow. 'You need peace and quiet now, Miss Granton. Whatever is worrying you, we'll try to sort it out for you.' She began to tidy up the bedclothes and placed the pillows flat on the bed. 'Lie down,' she urged. 'Get some rest. Things are always better after a good sleep.' The nurse turned to Saskia. 'You should go now.'

Chapter 20

In the dark watches of the night the herring 'swims' begin to ascend from the mid-water regions of the sea. Across the surface the bountiful plankton float with the currents. At the time of the full moon, stirred up by strong tides, millions of fish, shoal upon shoal, rise to feed.

Saskia rested her forehead against the window in the drawing room of Cliff House. On the surface of the water she could see gannets plunging, puffins riding the waves. Dusk was falling. Her own reflection was beginning to take shape in the window before her. It was not yet so clear an image as to identify her as Saskia. I could be Alessandra, thought Saskia, standing here, watching the sea. If I lived as long in this house, would I become so attached to it that to leave it even for one night would upset me?

'*She'll go crazy.*'

That's what Neil Buchan had said would happen if Alessandra was not allowed home from hospital. Saskia examined the word in her head. *Crazy*. No, Alessandra was not crazy. She had been mentally ill. She was still very emotionally fragile, but she was not crazy. And

147

anyway, 'crazy' was not a word to describe people who were sick in that way. A picture of Gideon's younger sister came to Saskia; the girl's stick-like arms, her pinched, thin face, becoming more gaunt as anorexia enclosed her mind in its vice. Gideon's sister wasn't crazy. She was unwell and needed treatment.

Knowing there was nothing else she could do tonight Saskia decided to take a bath. It would help unwind her after the trauma of the day. She turned from the window and her eyes caught sight of Alessandra's bureau lying open. As she reached over to close up the flap she saw a pile of papers there: Alessandra's cheque book, bank statements and receipts. Saskia pushed the papers into the bureau and closed it shut. She walked past the big table where the books, pamphlets, papers and maps lay spread out. Saskia stopped and, without thinking, sat down and pressed the PLAY button on the tape recorder. She heard Alessandra's voice, the beautiful melodic tones of the Northeast, asking the interview questions in her native tongue.

She was speaking to her own people.

As she had once done to Saskia.

Walking on the beach together, Alessandra talking, her voice textured like shot silk, a reprise of the sea itself and the rolling fertile land of the Northeast. The translucent shimmering phrases, the soft burr of the 'r' within the words, the rounding fullness of the vowel sounds.

'Ken now, little quine, Ah'll tell ye a tale of the mermaids who come an' sit on the rocks abune to comb their gowden hair and sing the sangs that sailors love to hear.'

But now Alessandra had ironed out her accent. When

Saskia had earlier reminded her great-aunt that she had spoken to her in the Doric as a child, and asked Alessandra why she never spoke like that now, Alessandra shook her head and said, 'I am better understood this way.' But even when quite small Saskia had understood Alessandra very well. Like any young child she was borne along, uplifted by the musicality of the language, riding high on the pounding surge of the story itself. Not to have this any more gave Saskia a keen sense of loss. Her fingers lingered on the tape recorder. Alessandra had done this consciously. But surely by deliberately eliminating her native speech Alessandra was eliminating part of her identity?

Saskia lifted her head. Now that it was fully dark outside, the room, reflected in the window, showed her a young woman sitting at a table, alone.

Was Alessandra trying to eradicate who she was? Always wearing the same black or grey clothes, her restrained manner, the careful use of language? Saskia thought of the way she herself spoke, how her sentences were constructed, and the way Neil Buchan formed his, and the difference between them. But Alessandra's way of talking was distinct from both of them; her speech had no natural rhythm, except here on the interview tapes or when telling Saskia of her youth. When Alessandra was speaking to her own people, she seemed more at ease, without fear.

Fear.

That was it! Saskia rewound the tape and played it again. She listened to the voice of her great-aunt. It was relaxed, whereas most other times, within the timbre of

Alessandra's voice was another note. Fear. Her aunt seemed to be in a constant state of fear.

There was Alessandra's manner of twisting her hands. Her way of walking, of holding herself, of watching, always alert. Was it she, Saskia, that Alessandra feared? No, it couldn't be. If it was, then her great-aunt would not have welcomed her to stay with her. Who then? Or what? Or ... where? Could it be places? Alessandra seemed to avoid certain places – the attic room, the beach near the far rocks, and the outside cellar, where she always stood near the door.

Saskia looked around her. Was it the house? Was Alessandra actually afraid of the house, and that was why she could not leave it? Had the house cast some kind of spell upon her? Well, now, she Saskia was alone in Cliff House tonight. Should *she* be afraid?

Saskia stood up. She was tired and possibly having a reaction to the accident and the upset at the hospital. She mustn't allow herself to be swamped by it all. She would have a bath – that would de-stress her and then she would sleep better.

As she ran the bath Saskia thought about her situation in the house. If she didn't want to be on her own, she could easily call Neil Buchan and ask him to take her to a local bed and breakfast. She wouldn't need to explain anything, just say that she was nervous by herself. But she *wasn't* nervous. She liked the house. It was a beautiful house and she could understand why her great-aunt would not want to leave it. Alessandra was entwined with the house as the house was with the cliff, the land with the sea.

Saskia stepped into the bath and stirred the water to make the bubble bath foam around her. She looked down at her body, glad that she could bear to do so now without flinching, that the years of embarrassing puberty were over. Those long months of tortuous evolving, the lack of choice as your hair, face, voice changed without giving notice, the seesaw swings from absolute confidence to earth-moving uncertainty, the search for self which she realized was still ongoing. She recalled the brief time Gideon and she had been together, both merely seeking some comfort from the barrenness of their home life, and both fortunately recognizing it almost at the same time, so that they had ended their relationship but managed to remain friends. He too was constrained to stay at home. He had submitted applications to local colleges and universities, saying that he couldn't leave because his parents provided too much good material for his writing. But later, when he and Saskia confided in each other, he had told her that it was for his little sister that he stayed behind. He wanted to wait until she was a bit older before leaving.

But she, Saskia, did not have that consideration. So what was keeping her at home? Love? Comfort? Selfish reasons? Her father had made it clear that he would withdraw financial support if she did not do what he wanted, that she would not benefit from the business if she was not prepared to take an active part in it. As she lay in the bath, the unfairness of that struck her. Before, she had always thought it a reasonable stance for him to take, but now it rankled slightly. Surely she should be able to choose? One or two friends were in similar circumstances. Ahmad's father was determined he would be a doctor as he was, and would sanction no other career plans from his son.

Saskia wrung out the facecloth, placed it over her eyes and slid down under the water. She had a vision of herself from above, hair floating free in the water. She who loved water would become part of it, poor drowned Saskia, like the fair Ophelia in the pre-Raphaelite painting pinned on the wall of the sixth-form common room. Saskia submerged her face. Water would bubble into her lungs and she would not care. The silkies would come to take her under the waves to the ocean floor. There she would lie, and passing mermaids would comb her hair. Behind Saskia's eyelids wide elongated ribbons of fire-flame unravelled: the northern lights inside her head.

From outside the house came a faint rustle. Saskia sat up quickly, water streaming from her. This upstairs bath-room was above the kitchen. If someone was at the back door she would have heard them knock. It must be shale running from the cliff.

Saskia got out of the bath. The water had become cold. She'd go downstairs and make herself a warm milky drink for bed. There was a towelling dressing gown hanging on the back of the bathroom door. Saskia looked at it for a moment or two before putting it on. It must belong to Alessandra. But her great-aunt had said that she didn't climb stairs . . . her arthritis . . . It was one of the reasons Alessandra had given for not going up to the attic . . .

Saskia thought about the accident this afternoon. It

seemed such a long time ago, not just a few hours. Alessandra couldn't have serious arthritis and ride a bicycle. She was almost as fit as Saskia, had been no more than a hundred metres behind her as she reached the top of the road this afternoon. And her great-aunt gardened and chopped wood with an axe. This hangnail of uncertainty about Alessandra was with Saskia as she went downstairs.

As she passed the phone in the hall it occurred to her she should tell her parents that Alessandra was in hospital.

'Oh, poor Alessandra,' said Saskia's mother at once. 'What a shock for her. I hope there's nothing else broken.' And then she added, 'Are you all right in that big house on your own, Saskia?'

'I'm fine,' said Saskia. 'It'll just be for one night.'

'Well if you change your mind just check into the hotel in the village.'

'I'll be fine, Mum. Stop fussing. I'm more concerned about Alessandra being in hospital.'

'It's probably a precaution in case she has a delayed reaction. I'll send her a card and maybe flowers to cheer her up. She had strange little ways but we got on all right.'

'How strange?' asked Saskia. 'I know she wasn't well for a while.'

'Oh, has she told you about that? Just her manner, I suppose, always watchful, never at ease. And . . . in the past she did a few odd things.'

'Like what?"

'She tore down all the curtains at one time, and your

153

father thinks she smashed things and burned them. He said his mother told him the house was full of beautiful furniture when he was young – oak chests, tables, ornate lamps, brass candlesticks. The last time he was there he went through all the rooms and a lot of the good stuff is gone.'

Saskia heard her father speaking close to her mother and then he came on the line. 'Are *you* all right, Saskia?' he asked, his voice sharp with anxiety. 'Your mother told me there had been an accident. I had to speak to you myself – she is so hopeless at telling me anything.'

Because you don't pay her any attention, thought Saskia. 'I'm OK,' she said.

'I'll fly up to Aberdeen. I'll come right now if you need me.'

Saskia smiled, knowing that her father was trying to be friendly after their argument about her summer job. She wondered what he'd do if she said, 'Yes, come, I need you.' Instead she said, 'Aunt Alessandra has a broken ankle, that's all.'

Saskia went to make a hot drink. Her parents had sounded concerned. Both of them had put their own selfishness to one side to enquire about her. That was comforting, and she felt better as she poured her mug of hot chocolate and took it through to the big room. In the right-hand corner of the window, on the cliff road, there was flash of car headlights. Saskia picked up the binoculars from the windowsill and put them to her eyes. A car had pulled in at the indent on the cliff road above the headland. She could only see the headlights. It was too dark for her to see the occupants of the car, but not, she realized, for anyone to see her. She was standing out-lined in the light of the drawing room. Feeling suddenly vulnerable, Saskia wrapped the towelling dressing gown closer and tied the belt more tightly.

Her mother telling her that Alessandra smashed things had unsettled her. There was certainly nothing of much value in the house; the furniture was sparse and func-tional. Had her great-aunt destroyed the rest of it in some kind of mad fit? Were Alessandra's careful move-ments those of a person hanging onto their self-control? The axe her aunt used to split kindling was embedded in the block of wood at the back door.

Saskia moved away from the window. She picked up her mug of hot chocolate and warmed her hands around it. From the garden came a small sputter of disturbed gravel. Saskia whirled round. Birds on the wall outside? Then another noise. This time Saskia was in no doubt about the sound. Someone was moving quietly on the gravel path around the house.

Chapter 21

Saskia's fingers clenched around her mug of hot chocolate. She fought down her fear and tried to think. If there was a prowler outside then she should phone the police. She stepped quietly into the hall. Then she heard a gentle tap on the front door and someone said her name.

'Who's there?' she called out.

'Neil. Neil Buchan.'

Saskia unlocked the front door. Neil Buchan stepped from the shadows.

Saskia felt faint.

Neil Buchan looked into her face. 'Sorry if I scared ye,' he said. 'I thought I'd walk along and ask how Miss Granton is. I saw a light on upstairs, but when I got to the house it had gone oot. I waited to see if ye were aboot, but when I didn't hear anything I decided to knock quietly and if ye didn't answer just go awa' again.'

'Come in,' said Saskia. She stood for a moment in the hall to recover herself and then led him into the drawing room. 'They've kept my great-aunt in overnight, and

156

what you said is true – she is extremely distressed about it.'

'I thought that might happen.' Neil looked at Saskia and then said cautiously. 'Years ago . . . there was a time when she didn't keep well.'

'I know,' said Saskia. 'Alessandra told me all about it.' Then she reflected to herself that, almost certainly, her great-aunt had not told her everything there was to know.

Neil nodded. 'Aye, well then, ye'll know that she was in a special hospital for a while?'

'Yes,' said Saskia.

'She's told you?'

'Bits of it,' said Saskia. 'She said that she used to sleep-walk right onto the beach. She was explaining to me why you were reassuring her that day I found the sick seal.'

'We get on fine. Tho' she's a proud woman, she'd never tak' help from a'body. Some winters I wondered that she survived, though I ken she's sold bits o' furniture to antique dealers.'

Saskia stared at Neil. 'I – we . . . I don't think my parents knew about that.'

'Well, now she's got her wee job at the Heritage Centre and that's been good for her in many ways.' Neil picked up one of the old photographs that was lying on the table. 'She's the perfect person to do this kind of work. Kens so much aboot the sea and the land. Some o' these photographs are from way before the last war but she kens a' aboot the old ways. That's my own father sitting there with the pipe in his mouth.'

157

Saskia took the photograph from Neil. 'Oh,' she said. 'I can see the likeness.' She glanced at Neil and then back to the photograph. 'Your features are so strong, your forehead, the shape of your face.'

Neil looked pleased. He pointed to the thick sweaters that all the men were wearing. 'What ye canna see properly in these black and white photographs is that each fisherman's gansey had a different pattern. Ye could almost tell the family name by the colour and the design. Sometimes it was the only way to identify a man if he'd been washed overboard and been in the sea a lang time.' Neil leaned over to look at a map spread out on the table. ' "The Lands of Buchan in Aberdeenshire",' he read out loud. 'They say that everybody in this area has a drop of Buchan blood. Such a ton of stuff she's kept. There must be mony a tale here for the telling. And she's the one that would ken how tae dae it. She a'ways had a good brain.'

'You've known her since she was small?'

'Aye. She was the finest-looking woman in these parts but nae body daured go near her for fear o' her father. A cruel hard man with a filthy temper. My own father was a strict parent, but John Granton had a dark side. When she went with the rest of the quines to follow the fishing, the boys were round her like a flock o' gulls following a boat.'

'She never told me anything about that,' said Saskia.

'She wisnae as dour as she is now, ye ken,' said Neil. 'She was a'fa' bonnie. Tall, fine features, with hair the colour of the setting sun. She'd tae keep awa' fae the harbour, mind, when the boats were due to sail. It's an old superstition. Even now mony a captain would turn back if they met a man with a beard or a quine with red hair. I'd come along to her hoose to keep her company when a'body else was doon at the harbour seeing them off.'

'You never went to sea?'

'I wanted to, to follow my father, an' his father, and his father's father.' Neil sighed. 'All drownded, bar me. I was lucky. My mother a'ways said that. The "lucky loon" she ca'd me. I was the last in the family, her only boy, an' when Ah was born Ah weighed nae mair than twa tatties, an' I wisnae breathing.

' "Git his coffin ready," the midwife said, "ye can tell that bairn's nae lang for this world." An' my mother began tae cry, and the midwife scolded her and said, "Ye ken fine the way it is, Kate. The Lord wills that some ye've tae gae back richt awa'."

'But my oldest sister, Chris, she was only thirteen, she took me and drapped me intae the basin fu' o' hot water. "The Lord can bide His time for this one," she said, "we're keepin' him here wi' us."

'An' then Ah let out a cry, an' even though the midwife thocht it blasphemy what my sister had said, she spat in my mouth an' there Ah was. They had to feed me with milk through an eye-dropper for the first few weeks. An' when I grew, they wouldna' let me gang tae the fishin'. The girls kept a' their money for me, and after the war they bought me an auld car. I learned tae drive an' began tae hire out, folk gaun tae Aberdeen, or weddings, or such like. An' that's a' Ah am today, a taxi driver.'

159

Neil looked out of the window to the sea in the darkness. 'Well, Ah'm alive, an' a lot that I grew up with arenae, but sometimes, when Ah hear the herring gulls cryin', an' Ah watch them follow the boats oot as they leave in the early morning . . . well . . .' Neil stopped and shrugged.

Saskia too looked out to the sea. 'It *is* dangerous though,' she said. 'And my father's family in particular appear to have suffered great loss. My father is very uneasy about the sea.' Saskia hesitated. 'He worries about me being too attached to it.'

Neil narrowed his eyes and said, 'Aye. If Ah was married and had a lass your age Ah might be that way too.'

Saskia looked at him. It suddenly seemed to her a reasonable apprehension on the part of her father to be concerned for her safety.

'Your father's father, Alessandra's brother Rob, was never found,' Neil went on, 'and that's a bad thing. There's nae death certificate, nae insurance for a sailor lost at sea. The family have to wait years before they can claim any compensation, and folk find it hard to grieve withoot a grave. At least with Alessandra's own father his body was washed up.'

'I thought he was lost at sea too,' said Saskia.

'He wisnae killed at the deep-sea fishing,' said Neil. 'He was collecting lobster pots one night and must hae got caught in a rip tide. His body came ashore further doon the coast but the boat was broken on the rocks at the headland.'

The rocks!

Ben had been right. There was a tragedy connected with those rocks.

'It's such a pity,' said Saskia. 'Alessandra's life seems to have been full of sorrow. Losing her father and her brother, and having no love of her own.'

'When she was a young woman she was fu' of life and laughter,' said Neil, 'fond o' bright colours, and . . . she did have a love o' her own. His name was Darach.'

'Darach?'

'Darach Keal. She met him when she was awa' at the herring wi' my twa sisters. Her father said he could marry her if he brocht him a thousand pounds dower. A thousand pounds! It might as well have been a million. But the lad reckoned he would dae it and he went awa' tae the whalin'. Up to the Arctic, but that was played oot, so he went off tae the South Seas, round about Japan an' the like. Ye could mak' big money in the whalin'.'

'How did you know about Darach?' Saskia asked Neil.

'Because the letters and the parcels cam' tae oor hoose. Chris and May, ma tae sisters, used to keep them safe for Alessandra. If they were delivered tae this hoose Alessandra's father wid a'ways open her letters and tak' her presents awa', so eventually she wrote tae Darach nae tae send the letters tae Cliff House but to send them tae us. She was fly enough though. So as nae tae gae the auld man any suspicions Darach had tae send aince every sae aften tae her at her ain hame.'

'And Darach never came back,' said Saskia sadly.

'Oh aye, he cam' back,' said Neil.

Saskia looked at him in surprise.

'He cam' back right enough, but she widnae hae him. He cam' back and for some reason, that very night she sent him awa'. An' he went awa'. Months and months went by, an' the next we heard aboot him was when the mission man was at her door. He had been drowned, like her father and her brother before him. The Grantons are a family that gave back more to the sea than they ever took from it.'

Chapter 22

The phone ringing in the hall woke Saskia the next morning. She glanced at her watch as she ran downstairs to pick it up. It was only just half past eight. Who would ring her so early?

It was the ward sister at the cottage hospital.

'What's wrong?' Saskia asked in alarm.

'Please don't worry. It is nothing too serious. We are transferring your great-aunt, Miss Granton, to Aberdeen. It turns out that the break is a complicated fracture and it might be better to put a pin in the leg. That would be done at the hospital there. She'll go by ambulance this morning.'

'How is she?' Saskia asked the sister. 'You know she was a bit distressed about having to stay in for even one night?'

'I can't say that she is very happy about it,' the sister replied.

Saskia wondered what level of anxiety that guarded remark covered.

Before she went upstairs to wash and dress Saskia checked the bus timetables. She decided she would catch the late-morning bus and get there for afternoon visiting. But first she should look out some more clothes for Alessandra. Her great-aunt would need some tops and a skirt or trousers to replace the ones she had been wearing.

Saskia went into Alessandra's room. She felt distinctly ill at ease at the prospect of opening the locked doors of her great-aunt's wardrobe. But Alessandra needed a change of clothing. She had no choice. Saskia unlocked the single door that had the key in the keyhole. The door swung open. On the hangers were several items – a blouse, cardigan, skirt, two pairs of trousers, all in black or dark grey. Were these all the clothes her great-aunt owned?

The double doors that made up the rest of the wardrobe were also locked. But the key she had in her hand would fit. Saskia put it in the lock, unlocked the other two wardrobe doors and pulled them open, and then she caught her breath.

Hanging like foliage in a rain forest were half a dozen garments in colours of blues and greens, and yellow and purple. From the depths of the wardrobe the materials shone out in the light from the window. Saskia parted the garments with her hands to look at them. There was a kimono of pale-yellow silk, an emerald-green high-necked shantung shift, split from ankle to thigh, a heavily embroidered jacket of dark-purple velvet with draped sleeves, the shimmering iridescence of a midnight-blue silken dressing gown with a red open-mouthed dragon embroidered on its back.

A row of shelves ran down one side, and on them,

singly and in small piles, lay exotic things: an ornamental brooch backed with mother of pearl, a decorated whale tusk, a beaded purse, slippers trimmed with pink flamingo feathers, paper parasols, ornate hair combs of amber and tortoiseshell.

Inside the purse was a letter.

'*Alessandra, my Alessandra . . .*'

Chapter 23

At the hospital in Aberdeen a nurse took Saskia to the ward sister's office.

'We would like to check some details about Alessandra Granton. She has named you as her nearest living relative.'

The ward sister read out her great-aunt's address. 'You stay there with her?'

Saskia hesitated. The word 'stay' in the sentence confused her slightly. It wasn't only the unique words of the Northeast that she had trouble understanding, the sentence construction and the placing of ordinary words within a phrase sometimes sounded foreign to her southern ears. By 'stay' they must mean 'live with'. Saskia thought quickly, and decided it was better if they thought that she lived with her aunt at Cliff House, otherwise her father's name and his contact details would go down as Alessandra's nearest living relative. Saskia instinctively felt that Alessandra would not want this. 'Yes,' she said. 'I do.'

'She says she has never been married, and that you are her great-niece and her nearest living relative?'

'Yes,' answered Saskia, now without any hesitation deliberately excluding her father.

'Your great-aunt has had health problems over the years,' the sister said cautiously. 'We think this is making her so much more anxious than she need be about a straightforward surgical procedure.'

'I know about this,' said Saskia. 'She spent some time in what I think was a psychiatric hospital and it makes her anxious about any hospital.'

'Yes . . . I've been reading her medical notes. But she has been at home for quite some time. Does she cope all right in the house?'

'Absolutely,' said Saskia firmly. 'Cooks, cleans, everything.'

'She is not bothered by the pain of her broken ankle or the prospect of an operation,' said the sister, 'yet . . . she appears frightened.'

'I wondered about that,' said Saskia. 'But I suppose if, at the time she was mentally ill, they had to forcibly take her into care for her own good then she would be scared it might happen again.'

The sister glanced down at Alessandra's medical notes. 'She wasn't sectioned.'

'Sorry?'

'Your great-aunt wasn't taken against her will to the psychiatric hospital. She admitted herself. She could have left at any time.'

'Oh,' Saskia faltered. 'I just assumed . . .'

'Mental illness is so misunderstood,' said the sister. 'Much of it is closely related to duress. Nearly all of us, at some time, have almost more than we can cope with.

Some mental illness is merely the mind breaking down under extreme stress. And those of us who do manage to cope, instead of having sympathy with those who can't, tend to isolate them. The community at large tends to avoid those who are mentally ill.'

'She has been on her own quite a lot,' said Saskia, 'and I know that she has had bad dreams.' She hesitated and then asked, 'She wouldn't break things?'

'Her illness would not make her violent. Why do you ask?'

Saskia shifted uncomfortably in her chair. 'Oh, you know . . . family stories.'

'She's certainly extremely distressed at being moved from the cottage hospital,' said the sister, 'but we've given her something to calm her nerves. I spent a long time talking to her this morning, and she's agreed to remain for a few days and let us treat her.'

Alessandra's eyes watched Saskia as she approached down the ward.

'Don't worry,' she said, as Saskia took a chair beside her bed. 'I am not going to make a fuss today. I am sorry I was overwrought yesterday. I do get nervous about things.'

'It's all right,' said Saskia. 'I'd hate to be in hospital.'

'The ward sister is very good,' said Alessandra. 'She has persuaded me to stay here for another day or two. She is a compassionate woman.'

'I'm sure that the doctors and nurses understand that bereavement would have made you . . . fragile . . . for a while.'

Alessandra smiled gently at Saskia. 'Such a polite understatement shows you are from the south, Saskia. I was more than "fragile". I was deranged, completely mentally unwell for many months . . . years.' Alessandra looked sideways at Saskia. 'Possibly still am, a little.'

'Neil came by last night to ask after you and see that I was all right,' said Saskia. 'He explained a few things.'

'He has been kind to me over the years,' said Alessandra. She studied Saskia's face. 'He would tell you about Darach?' And as Saskia gave a little nod, Alessandra continued, 'He would not tell you the part he played in all of it. His mother kept chickens and he brought me my letters hidden in the eggs. When I was ill he came and fed me. He left food at my door. He is a good man.'

'He told me you grew up together,' said Saskia.

'He was younger than I was by five years but he used to trail after me and his older sisters to try and join in our games. When he was small we treated him mercilessly, wrapping him up in shawls and wheeling him about in a little cart when we played house. Later, us three girls decided to be princesses together and he was our faithful pageboy. When May and Chris were old enough to follow the fishing fleet away to the gutting, I was queen and he my bravest knight. With his clothes-pole lance he would joust among the washing lines and slay dragons for me.'

And is still doing it, thought Saskia.

'When I was about fourteen or fifteen,' Alessandra went on, 'he was about eleven or twelve. He would follow me around wherever I went, bringing me clams and mussels from the shore to help me bait the hooks. Then he was thirteen and we would meet on the top road and he'd give me my letters from Darach. It was very brave of him. Both my father and his would have thrashed him thoroughly if they'd caught him. Strange that he did it because I never gave him even a penny. I had no money.'

A parcel of slow understanding began to unwrap itself in Saskia's mind. Neil Buchan. Neil who had never married. She recalled how Neil had lingered in the garden when he had first brought her to Cliff House, his eyes on the face of her great-aunt as he spoke to her.

'He didn't do it for money,' she said gently.

'Why then?' asked Alessandra.

'For love,' said Saskia. 'He was in love with you as a boy,' and, as the obvious fact entered her head, Saskia continued, 'He still is.'

'Neil Buchan!' exclaimed Alessandra.

'Yes,' said Saskia. She looked with close attention at her great-aunt. 'And you know it.'

Alessandra glanced away. 'You imagine things, child. You did it when you were little. You are doing it now.'

Saskia thought carefully about what she should say next. 'Aunt Alessandra,' she said, 'I am not little any more. I am no longer a child.'

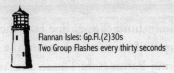

Flannan Isles: Gp.Fl.(2)30s
Two Group Flashes every thirty seconds

Chapter 24

Saskia left the hospital and walked into the city centre. It occurred to her that Ben might be working in his office today and she stopped and asked someone the way to the Marine Research Institute.

When she got there the girl at reception said he was down at the docks. 'You'd have to nail Ben's feet to the floor,' she laughed, 'to get him to stay indoors for long.' She waved her hand towards the office area. 'Just go through and leave a note on his desk. He'll probably call you when he returns.'

Ben's desk by the window was a jumble of papers, scientific reports, professional journals with articles highlighted, a few cups with congealing coffee, and above it the best poster Saskia had seen in a long time. It was a black and white photograph of a Native North American with a caption that read:

> *Only after the last tree has been cut down,*
> *Only after the last river has been poisoned,*
> *Only after the last fish has been caught,*
> *Only then will you find that money cannot be eaten.*

The Marine Institute was at one end of the city and as Saskia left the building she saw a sign pointing to the preserved fishing cottages at Fitdee. She turned in that direction and walked through the narrow lanes until she came to the open place where the posts for drying the nets still stood. What had once been a tiny village was now overtaken by the city, but the layout of the buildings and the stone walls of the houses held fast to their own identity.

Saskia wandered down towards the harbour. On a steep slope within sight of the sea she found the Fisheries Museum and went inside. There was a model of a fisher-girl standing by a trough piled with herring. Her fingers were wrapped with cloth strips and at once Saskia thought of her great-aunt and Neil's two sisters. She entered a tiny booth and watched a grainy film about herring drifters. The tremendous difficulties and hardness of the men's lives were apparent, and yet Saskia saw that they were smiling as they worked about their boat. She thought of the old fisherman whom she'd heard speaking on Alessandra's tape, the soft sound of contentment in his voice. She remembered Neil Buchan looking out to sea from the window in her aunt's house and telling of his sisters' decision that he would not go to the fishing, unable to conceal the undertone of regret.

Saskia found some albums with old photographs of fishing communities and in among them was one taken at the harbour in Fhindhaven. Was her grandfather one of these young men lined up beside the boat? Laughing into the camera, shy, yet pleased at having their picture taken. She asked one of the museum guides. No names, sorry. But we could try to trace them. No, no thanks, she said and told him that she'd be in Fhindhaven for the summer.

'Then you could do no better than the Fhindhaven Heritage Centre, or the one in Buckie. The staff there have tremendous local knowledge and phenomenal memories. I can give you some contacts.'

But she already had the contacts. She knew the people to ask – one in particular was closely related to her. And that was just what she was going to do, Saskia decided. As soon as Alessandra was home from hospital and well enough, she was going to find out everything she could about her own family history.

In a side room there was a small exhibition on the whaling industry. Saskia shuddered at the description of how the whales were lashed to the side of the boat, the skin stripped off and the blubber removed. One of the glass cases displayed silver snuff boxes, examples of scrimshaw, the long spiral tusk of a narwhal, and the record of a Greenland whaler's diary.

The thrashing beast broke the back of the ship and with a heaving crack the mast fell. The harpooners in the whaleboats were dragged down and we never saw a one of them again. With what provisions we could salvage and carrying the last small boat between us we took to the ice . . .

With the mate McLeod . . . an evil man with a foul mouth, but with a compass in his head, he will lead us, like Moses, out of our affliction.

> *Open water before us. Prepared the boat,*
> *raised a sail and laid in a course.*
> *By guess and by God, we hope to see our*
> *families once more.*

It was like a scene from *Moby Dick*, thought Saskia, and then smiled at herself. *Moby Dick* had been taken *from* life, not the other way round.

Coming out of the Fisheries Museum, she bumped into Ben.

'Aha,' he said with a grin. 'I found your note on my desk and I thought you might be here.'

'Really?' Saskia was flattered. She noticed that he was slightly out of breath. Had he run all the way from the Marine Institute to meet her? 'I was catching up on some of the local history.'

'You would have walked past the fisher cottages at Fitdee on your way down?' Ben asked.

Saskia nodded.

'Did you see how the houses face in to each other? They were built like that to protect them against the elements, but of course it also draws a community closer together.'

'Fitdee . . .' said Saskia. 'Is it called that because we are beside the river Dee? Foot of the Dee?'

'Well done!' said Ben. 'We'll have you speaking the language yet.'

'I guess that's why this city is named Aberdeen,' said Saskia.

'Gosh, you're a good student!' Ben laughed. ' "Aber" is old British for river mouth, so yes, Aberdeen is the mouth of the river Dee.'

Saskia felt ridiculously pleased by his praise.

'What brings you into the big city today?' He looked at her closely. 'Everything OK?' he asked.

'Not totally,' said Saskia. And as they walked together along the sea front she told him of the accident and then of Alessandra's anxiety at being in hospital.

'Even though she is your great-aunt she is only in middle age,' said Ben. 'She's not a really old lady, so she'll have a bit more resilience. You're not too worried about her, are you?'

'Not so much now,' said Saskia. 'The nurses have calmed her down quite a lot. She's had terrible tragedy in her life, and she gets a bit fraught from time to time.'

'I was aware that she was quite sensitive the first time we met,' said Ben. 'The day you found the seal on the beach she seemed more than a little upset.'

And you were so considerate and kind, thought Saskia. She glanced at Ben. His face showed concern. It occurred to her that kindness was an important element in a relationship.

'Let me run you home,' said Ben. 'I can make an excuse to go up to Fhindhaven and it means you won't have to take the bus.'

'I'll need to do some shopping first,' said Saskia. 'I want to get Alessandra a few magazines to read.'

'Fine,' said Ben. 'And if your great-aunt has to stay in hospital for a few days then you might have to put off beginning work for a bit – I can fix that for you, so don't worry about it. And, worse, we might have to cancel our date for the cinema this weekend, so why don't we buy some food and I'll make a barbecue on your beach?'

'A barbecue?' said Saskia. She had buttoned up her jacket as they were walking. 'I know it is quite a pleasant day, but isn't it a bit cold for a barbecue?'

'Not at all,' said Ben. 'If you are going to spend any more time than just a few weeks' holiday up here then you'd better get used to dealing with the weather. Come on, let's go.' He grabbed her hand and began to run, pulling Saskia with him. 'You can have a barbecue on the beach at any time as long as it's not actually blowing a blizzard.' He laughed. 'And even then . . .'

'You're joking!' cried Saskia, trying to keep up with him. 'You don't have barbecues in snow.'

'Have done,' said Ben. 'We only give in when it gets to storm-force gales.'

In Saskia's opinion, it practically *was* a storm-force gale. Ben had made a makeshift windbreak in the shelter at the foot of the stairs that led onto the beach at Cliff House, but halfway through the preparations Saskia went inside to find a warmer jacket and some gloves.

On her return she paused for a few minutes at the top of the beach steps and watched him building the fire. He was so assured in what he did and said. He'd found his place in life, had fixed on a purpose that would both extend and fulfil him, while she . . . she seemed to be directed by circumstance and the whim of others. If she had not come to visit her great-aunt she might now be working for her father and preparing for a university course that did not suit her.

Ben glanced up and waved. Saskia waved back, but she took her time as she went down the stairs to join him. He *was* very attractive and she enjoyed his company, but this time, she decided, she was not going to rush into things. It was easy to be flattered by the attention of someone. She recalled a quote from some novelist whose work she had studied in English literature. 'Love is complete attention,' this writer had said. That wasn't the whole truth, thought Saskia. You could be deceived by attention, seduced, so that your own will became suppliant under the force of another's. If a relationship developed between her and Ben, it would be because *she* wanted it to, as much as he might.

'Sorry to be a wimp,' she said as rejoined him on the beach, 'but I was freezing.'

Ben put his arm around her and pulled her nearer. 'Don't apologize,' he laughed. 'It means we have to huddle together for warmth.' He bent and kissed the top of her head. 'Such beautiful hair,' he murmured.

Saskia tilted her head back and met his gaze. Her pulse and heartbeat had moved up a pace, but she didn't lean towards him, only put her head on one side and smiled at him. Ben cupped her face in his hands and they kissed lightly.

'That was long overdue,' he said.

Saskia stepped back. She punched him playfully on the arm. 'Oh yeah?'

'For my part,' said Ben, 'I felt like kissing you the first day I saw you, when you so gallantly agreed to help me carry half a hundredweight of sick seal along the beach.

'That's not a very romantic reason,' said Saskia.

He looked at her keenly. 'Would you have appreciated romance at that moment?'

'Probably not,' Saskia agreed.

'I wanted you to stay on for the summer so that I could get to know you better,' he went on, 'but the day we went to the fish market at Peterhead I sensed that you were beginning to make your own decisions about what you would and wouldn't do.'

Saskia smiled at Ben more happily now. It seemed that he understood without her having to spell it out.

When the food had been eaten and the fire was falling into a red glow they went down to the water and walked along the shore. On the skyline a solitary trawler headed home.

'I've been told the local fishermen used Cliff House to locate their fishing grounds,' said Saskia. 'They called it "finding the mark". I'd never heard that expression before.'

'It's a bit like dead reckoning,' said Ben, 'where you can estimate where you are by where you've been. It's an old form of navigation, but still effective.'

'Do you think the regulations that are in place now will protect the fishing grounds for the future?' Saskia asked Ben.

'Truthfully, no,' he replied. 'Not unless something is done to curb industrial fishing. I think the biggest problem is the destruction of the nursery areas and the species at the beginning of the food chain. And as some of those catches are destined to be turned into fish meal for fertilizer or to feed pigs and cattle it seems to be a tremendously wasteful use of resources.'

'Doesn't it get you down?' asked Saskia.

Ben grinned. 'I try to find ways to take my mind off it.'

He stopped walking and took both her hands in his. This time Saskia did not move away from him. He placed her arms around his own neck and bent his head and kissed her again.

Saskia leaned her head on his chest. She said, 'I loved your poster – the one above your desk.'

'I got it in California,' said Ben. 'I spent some time there on a whale watch. If only we were able to co-ordinate marine programmes around the world we could make changes that really matter.' He paused and then said fiercely, 'We *must* do it.'

Saskia looked up and saw passion and conviction on his face. She tightened her arms around him and held him close.

Chapter 25

Saskia waited until Ben had left and then phoned her parents. It was her father who answered.

'Transferred to a hospital in Aberdeen? Why? Is there something else wrong with Alessandra? Does she know who you are?'

'Of course she knows who I am,' said Saskia impatiently. 'She's broken her ankle, not had a stroke or anything.'

'When old people get a shock like that it can sometimes push them over the edge.'

Saskia recoiled from the implication in his voice.

'Perhaps I should come up? It may be that the time has come for her to leave Cliff House. Better to do it now while she's in hospital. You'd need a hand to sort out her things.'

Saskia thought of her father going through Alessandra's clothes, her books, her papers, rummaging around the house. On behalf of her aunt she felt affronted and had a strong desire to protect Alessandra. But she knew she would need to be careful how she spoke to her father. It might suit him to fly up and take over. She mustn't provoke him by yelling or going into a huff. She would be as devious as he.

'Ah,' she said, giving herself time to think. 'Let me talk to her doctor and ask her how long they intend keeping her there and I'll call you back.'

'Good girl, Saskia. My best girl. I knew I could rely on you.'

Rely on her to do what? Why did he himself not speak directly to her great-aunt? It came to Saskia's mind that a lot of the negative stories about Alessandra had come from her father.

'Dad, why don't you like your aunt Alessandra?' she asked him. 'Is it because I was sick after staying here when I was younger? It wasn't her fault that I was ill, you know. It was months after we came home from our holiday here that I got meningitis.'

'I know. I know. I was getting mixed up when I said that.'

'There is another reason, isn't there?'

'I don't want to talk about it.'

'Daddy, I'd like to know. Why do you hate her?'

'I don't hate her.'

'What is it then?'

'I don't know . . . she unsettles me.'

'Why?' said Saskia. 'She's been ill, but she's not a violent person.'

'I didn't think she was *violent*,' said her father. 'I wouldn't have let you visit her if I thought she was dangerous in any way.'

A sudden thought passed through Saskia's mind. 'Was that why we didn't come back after I was six years old?

Did you think she had done something to me, frightened me in some way?'

'No, not at all. She was very fond of you.'

'Neil Buchan says that she sold furniture over the years in order to live.'

There was a silence.

Saskia spoke again. 'Did you hear me, Dad? The furniture and the lamps that you thought Alessandra destroyed, she sold them. She needed the money.'

Saskia's father spoke slowly. 'No, no, that can't be right.' Then he added, 'One year I found the family baby cradle in bits in the cellar, and when other pieces of furniture disappeared I made an assumption. I shouldn't have done that. It's taken me a long time to overcome my dislike of her.'

'But *why* did you dislike her, Dad?'

'Because of what she did to me and my mother, but especially my mother.'

'Was this when you were very small?'

'Yes, but I remember it so clearly.'

'What do you remember?'

'I heard . . . I heard her say—' Her father's voice broke off.

With shock, Saskia realized that her father was genuinely distressed.

'Please tell me, Daddy.'

'I don't remember anything about the time I spent there as a baby,' said Saskia's father, 'except that my mother always said she was happy in that house. But she said we weren't there for very long. My mother said Alessandra suddenly told her to get out and take me with

182

her, so we had to go and live in Yarmouth. We were with my mother's relations there for years and years, until I was nearly thirteen and my mother married again. It was awful, so overcrowded.

'Later, when she thought about it, my mother wondered if Alessandra was upset that she'd never had a child. I think my mother was right. Alessandra was jealous that her sister-in-law had a baby and she didn't. That's why the cot was smashed up in the cellar, why she sent us away. She could not bear to see us so happy together. She was in love with a young man, a whaler, and he was supposed to come back and marry her, but he never did. My mother said there were lots of rumours that he had come back for her and Alessandra turned him down, sent him away, but I think he jilted her. He came back, saw what she was like, and chickened out of marrying her. Who can blame him? By all accounts he was a nice boy, one of those gentle folk that you find in the Western Isles. Anyway, I think, to save her face, he let it be said that she turned him down, but it couldn't have been that. She was waiting for him. Almost desperate, my mother said. He'd sent her presents and letters, but I think she destroyed all of them.'

No, she didn't, Saskia thought. I have seen them. In Alessandra's wardrobe. She'd kept them. For all those years. She must have loved him.

'Anyway,' her father went on, 'at some point, Alessandra went completely loopy, didn't eat for days and eventually they carted her off. She was right out of it for a bit but then she quietened down. She was lucky. She got a good doctor; he said she needed to be home.

They gave her day care and a home visitor. The district nurse called in from time to time, said she'd to re-learn everything, how to dress herself even. Lots of things she couldn't remember, but with Alessandra you never know if it was the treatment or whether it's what she chooses not to remember.

'We didn't hear a thing about this when it was happening. My mother hadn't a clue. Didn't even know the old man, my grandfather, had died until much later. He was dead and buried and Alessandra hadn't let us know. When I was about four or five we travelled north to visit Alessandra. My mother thought if we surprised her that Alessandra would welcome us in. My mother was so excited, telling me of her happy times in the big house, and how it was going to be again. The games we'd play in and out of all the rooms. I'd have a beach of my very own. We would make sandcastles together and I would sail on the sea in my own little boat. When we got there, Alessandra slammed the door in our faces. She told my mother never to come to Cliff House again.'

Saskia heard the break in her father's voice. After a moment or two she said gently, 'I'm really sorry if this is making you sad, Daddy, but please tell me the rest.'

Saskia's father coughed. Then he said grudgingly, 'I see now that she was probably mentally ill but it is one of my most awful childhood memories. Alessandra would not even let us into Cliff House. My mother stood outside, sobbing her heart out, begging. "Alessandra! Alessandra!" she called out. Even now I can see my mother's face, hear her voice. It frightened me so much. On the train she cried all the way home. I had to sit and watch her.'

Saskia's heart contracted. Pity for her father was such an unfamiliar emotion that she scarcely recognized it.

'When I was thirteen,' her father continued, 'my mother remarried. My stepfather was in the army and being posted all over the world, so we didn't know what was happening in Fhindhaven, though my mother always tried to keep in touch. Every time we moved she would write, in case Alessandra had lost her address. But Alessandra never replied. Eventually Neil Buchan sent a note and explained a few things. I got married, and when you arrived my mother made me promise that I would visit Alessandra and heal the rift between us. By that time my mother was dying. I couldn't refuse her.

' "She will love her brother's grandchild," my mother said. "I promise you. She will love Saskia." '

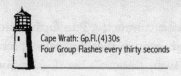

Chapter 26

Surface sea water, cooled by the massive ice caps at the North and South Poles, sinks down in the Arctic and Antarctic Oceans. Lighter warmer waters flow in from the Tropics to replace it. Currents move through the very deepest parts of the ocean . . .

The next morning Saskia's head was achy. She had not slept at all well, waking every so often with a start, imagining strange sounds in the attic above her head, dreaming of harpoons tipped in blood, and monstrous sea creatures washed up on strange-shaped rocks. She drew back the curtains at her bedroom window and stood looking out. For the first time since she had been at Cliff House, she felt the presence of the cliff as oppressive, the cries of the sea birds disturbing. She pulled on some clothes and went out to walk on the beach.

Crumpled near the far rocks she found the blanket with which she had covered the seal. The changing tides must have brought it back. Now Saskia knew why Alessandra was anxious about these rocks. It was where her own father's boat had been caught and crushed.

Saskia looked further round at where the cliff overhung the headland. No wonder Alessandra feared this place and did not want anyone walking near to it.

Just as Saskia returned to the house Neil Buchan phoned and Saskia brought him up to date on Alessandra's condition. 'She is more settled than she was before. I think she appreciates that if she doesn't let them fix her ankle she might have problems walking and cycling so she has resigned herself to it.'

'Are you visiting today?' he asked her.

'Of course,' said Saskia.

'I'll take you there if you like. I'm going that way anyway.'

Saskia smiled and said she'd wait for him at the end of the path.

In the car on the way to Aberdeen, Saskia told Neil about her conversation with her father the previous evening. 'You said Darach Keal came back for Alessandra. My father thinks that he came back to tell her he didn't want to marry her, that it was Darach who broke off their engagement. Did he? Or did he come back, but she sent him away?'

'Who knows?' Neil shrugged. 'By that time both of my sisters had married and were living elsewhere, and they were the only ones Alessandra would have told. But later when we talked about it together they couldn't believe that Alessandra sent Darach away, she loved him too much. But the gossips said that Darach had not enough money, and that as Alessandra would have her father's wealth she didn't need him. Darach wrote at least one more letter though, because I took it to her myself.'

'My grandmother Esther was still living in Cliff House with my father at the time?'

'Yes. But it was not long after Darach left that Alessandra told Esther that she didn't want her or her baby, your father, at Cliff House any more. Alessandra is supposed to have been so nasty to them both that Esther was forced to leave. That was strange. Esther was her brother Rob's wife, her own sister-in-law, but Alessandra sent them away, told them to leave the house and never come back. In the village they said that Alessandra wanted to be sure that she would have all the money to herself when her father died, although Esther was entitled to the house. If not all, then half of it at least.' Neil shook his head. 'I've not thought on it for a long time, but even now it does not seem a thing that Alessandra would do.'

'Perhaps the death of my grandfather – her brother – Rob affected her in some way?' suggested Saskia.

Neil sighed heavily. 'It was a sore blow. And yes, she grieved deeply for him. But for all that I don't think she should have sent the bairn and its mother away. They were her only living kin, and her brother had looked out for her for many years.'

'When you say "the bairn", you mean my father, don't you?' asked Saskia.

Neil nodded.

'He says he was about five years old the second time Alessandra sent them away.'

'That would be about right,' said Neil. 'The first time he and his mother left he was only a small thing. They came back again a few years later. By that time old Mr

Granton, Alessandra's father, had died and she had gone a bit funny . . . Wouldn't let anyone into the house.' Neil paused. 'Not even me.'

At the hospital a doctor spoke to Saskia.

'We will put the pin in Miss Granton's leg tomorrow morning. I want to have it done as soon as possible. She's eating very little and we are having to sedate her to contain her anxiety.'

'How soon can she come home?' asked Saskia. 'I think being in hospital is upsetting her.'

'I agree. Though the nurses say she is no trouble as a patient.'

'I think she might be pining for her house,' said Saskia. 'She has lived there since she was born. It is right by the sea.'

The doctor, a young woman, went to the window and looked towards the harbour. Her accent was Midlands. 'I can appreciate that. I came here to do my internship five years ago and never left. It is the light, and the sound, and the smell, and when you look out to the east you see. . .'

'The rim of the world,' said Saskia.

Silhouetted against the pillows Alessandra's face was shadowed and vulnerable. Without considering her action, Saskia reached out and took her hand. Alessandra looked down at their hands lying one on top of the other on the bedcover. Saskia felt her great-aunt's hand tremble within her own but Alessandra did not withdraw.

'I am afraid . . . now . . . of what might happen.'

It wrenched Saskia to watch Alessandra struggling

to tell her something without using the actual words.

'I know,' said Saskia, and she did know, without fully understanding. She knew that there was some particular fear that worried her great-aunt, some other desperate unhappiness that was part of Alessandra's life.

'There are things that I thought I should never tell anyone,' said Alessandra. 'And although I did not want to trouble him, I need to make things right between myself and your father. There is a chasm between us.'

'It is not just about you not lending him more money,' said Saskia. 'That's not what really upsets him.'

Alessandra lifted her head to look at Saskia.

'When my father was very young, you twice sent him and his mother away from Cliff House. He thinks that . . . that you did not like them.'

Alessandra stared at her. 'Child, I adored your father.'

'Was it your sister-in-law then?' Saskia persisted. 'Esther? Did you and she have an argument?'

'I loved her,' said Alessandra. 'She was like my brother, gentle, kind and good, and your father was a beautiful boy with red-gold hair. When your father was very young Esther went off to stay with her own people.'

'But my father says it was you who made her go. On two occasions you told them to leave. His mother told him this. The first time when he was small, and then again some years later, when they came back to visit you and you would not open the door. You did not even allow them to enter the house. He remembers his mother crying that time. You sent them both away.'

'It was the time of my madness when your grand-mother Esther brought your father to visit me as a small boy,' said Alessandra. 'That was why I would not let them in the house. At that time I could bear to have no one with me. Esther eventually understood that. She forgave me. I know that she forgave me because she came back a third time.'

'A third time?' said Saskia. 'My father did not mention that.'

'Your father knows nothing about that visit. Nor your mother. Esther came to see me not long after you were born. She brought you with her. I opened the door one morning and she was there. She stood upon my doorstep and placed you in my arms.'

' "Alessandra," she said, "I've brought Rob's grand-bairn for you to see."

'And I loved you in that instant, although I could see no resemblance at all to my brother.

' "There's no likeness until you see her wakened," said Esther.

'And, at the sound of her voice, you opened your eyes and I saw what she meant. You were your own person but you had the look of Rob. And Esther and I both began to cry, and so did you, and we had to stop to comfort you, and then we laughed. We laughed a lot, and I began to heal a little. She had not told your mother or father that she was taking you north to see me. Perhaps it was wrong of her. Your parents had left you in her care and gone off for a weekend. Your mother was unwell for months after your birth and was glad of a break. Esther drove north in one day and then back down the next. She did it because she knew she was dying.

' "My time has almost run out and I thought I'd do

191

one last thing for you, Alessandra, after all you did for me," Esther said.

' "I did nothing for you," I whispered.

' "Oh, yes you did, my sister. It is only now as I look back and think about events in the past I begin to suspect that I may have been in great danger. Even I do not know how much you did. But I thank you. I thank you for welcoming me to your house and your heart, and keeping me safe," she said.'

Safe.

'What did she mean?' asked Saskia. 'Was this when my father was not much more than a baby? When you were all so happy living together in Cliff House before your father died? You told me that my grandmother was frail, that Esther's health was poor. That wasn't true, was it? Why *did* you send them away then?'

'You do things for the best of reasons and are misunderstood,' said Alessandra.

A tear like a fish scale glittered on her cheek.

Chapter 27

Alessandra lay back on the pillow with her eyes closed. Saskia wondered if she should leave quietly and allow her some rest. As she moved in her chair her great-aunt spoke again without opening her eyes.

'I have never spoken of this to anyone.'

'Perhaps now you should,' said Saskia.

Esther sleeps, her head thrown back, lips parted, the baby by her side. The baby's face is flushed, breath milky-sweet.

The shadows in the house move and then don't move. The light from the sea, the moon on the water, the pull of the tide spreads across the windows. Silence, but not. My hand is on the wall of the house. Behind it is the cliff. Its weight will crush me.

I cannot watch over them every single night.

Golden child.

If you love them, let them go. Before it is too late.

'At first I did not see how my father looked at Esther.

'We put the grief of my brother's death behind us, and the baby, Sandy, thrived, sturdy and happy. Your father was a placid toddler, and as he grew out of the baby

193

stage my father said that he should have a room of his own. My father could be so charming when he chose. Esther took his advice, and soon Sandy was in a separate room.

'She did not know what was festering in my father's mind. And neither did I. I would have considered it an unspeakable wickedness to even consider such an idea.'

'One night I awoke and heard voices.

'It was my father.

'In Esther's bedroom.

'His room was on the ground floor. He said he'd been sleepwalking, not properly woken up, and had become confused. Esther was awake, although not frightened. She was too good to think what he might do. I heard their voices and came to see what was amiss. As he left her room he avoided my gaze. But I saw his look and it made me uneasy.

'It happened once more. He said he heard the child cry out.

'But if he heard the child cry, why did he go into her room when the baby was in the other? Still Esther did not think ill of him. Then I began to notice things. How during the day he contrived to catch her alone. In the evenings I saw him watching her and his attention was not benign. There was hunger in his eyes. I was deeply shamed by my thoughts and could tell no one what I suspected. I persuaded Esther to put the child's cot back in her room at night, thinking it might protect her. I was wrong. Again I heard him entering her bedroom, and this time I stopped him as he was at her bed, in the very act of drawing back the covers. For a moment I thought he would strike me and continue, but I managed to turn him away. She did not awaken.

'I did not go to bed that night nor any other after.

'By day I guarded her as best I could, but I knew that he would not give up. He was a man who took what he wanted, who had always had his own way in all things. At night I dared not sleep. I heard him prowl the house. I knew that if it continued I should go mad.

'I suggested that she should take her child to visit her own folk in Yarmouth. At the train station, just as the train was leaving, I told her not to come back.'

Muckle Flugga: Fl.(2)W20s
Two Flashes White every twenty seconds

Chapter 28

Saskia wondered how her father would react to Alessandra's explanation of her treatment of his mother. He needed knowledge of this part of his own family history, but not just now, Saskia decided, and not from her. It would help him to know that his great hurt had been caused by his aunt protecting his mother. He would surely understand then that what Alessandra had done had been prompted by love, not hate or jealousy, and that she had been unable to tell Esther or anyone else about it at the time.

And . . . there was more. Saskia was sure of this.

Alessandra had been ready to fall asleep when Saskia left the hospital. And Saskia had not encouraged her great-aunt to talk for any longer than she had done. She would wait until Alessandra was home and rested and then see if she wanted to tell her anything else.

Neil stood beside his taxi as Saskia came out of the hospital. He looked at her carefully as she walked towards him in the car park. He held the door open for her but said nothing, asked her nothing. She was glad of the silence. It meant that on the journey home she had the chance to rethink her attitudes. She saw that her own original perception of Alessandra was based on the opinion of others.

Her mother had made an assumption about Alessandra when she had said, 'She destroys things.' No. Saskia thought more carefully, picking out in her mind what she was trying to deduce to herself. Her *mother* had not made the assumption. Her mother had joined in with what her *father* had assumed. They knew, or saw something, part of a truth, and came to conclusions. Why? Why did people do that? It wasn't only her parents who did this. People assumed things. They heard what they wanted to hear, sometimes shaping the truth to fit in with their own needs of the moment. Alessandra, who had been ill, who had been mentally frail, became like many others, a victim of this type of thinking. And Alessandra, and people like her, didn't help their own case by not conforming. By refusing, or being unable, to live within the tribe, their eccentric behaviour ostracized them. The night after the accident, when Alessandra had been detained in the cottage hospital, Saskia herself had almost succumbed to following that way of thinking. Alone in Cliff House, she'd been on the verge of imagining the worst possible things about her great-aunt. Had experienced panicky fear, because when her mother had said that Alessandra smashed things, her own thoughts had made a connection with the axe Alessandra kept by the kitchen door.

Saskia saw Alessandra's house as Neil drove the car down the last stretch of the coast road towards Fhindhaven. Cliff House. The fishermen of Buchan had used it to find their mark. Saskia's own points of reference were dissolving as she experienced the remorseless unwinding of the blindfold of childhood. School was finished, and with it the guidance of teachers; friends were scattered, taking with them the support of her peer group; her parents revealed as fallible. Saskia stood in the hall. She looked at her hands. They were shaking.

Something was happening within her mind. A thought was speeding towards her, and she was terrified of its arrival. Her body started to react, her breath coming in short gasps. She needed to eat or drink something. Drink something. Hot tea. Saskia put the kettle on, moving restlessly about the kitchen as she waited for it to boil. She was feeling this way because of the stressful hospital visit, she told herself.

Taking a mug from the cupboard, a brown mug, carefully, she made herself some tea and added sugar. That was supposed to help with shock, and she could feel trauma beginning to mount.

Saskia tried to make her mind slow down. But this thought was not to be denied access. She gripped the edge of the kitchen worktop, trying to analyse what was happening. What had triggered this reaction within her? She had been thinking about her father being rejected by Alessandra.

And the thought was familiar. That was it. She recognized this particular panic: despair and hopelessness furring up inside her, rendering her arms and legs unable to function. And it was connected to another incident in her childhood. She had felt like this when she had been ill with meningitis.

No. It had begun earlier. *Before* the meningitis.

Like the fins of a fan concealing the picture hidden within, unseen until spread wide, the concertina of her memory unfolded.

She is on a train. Going home to London after the last holiday at Cliff House.

Her father has hurt his hand. Her parents are talking about how angry her father had been with Alessandra. They think her asleep. Then her mother goes to the toilet.

'What were you saying about Great-aunt Alessandra?' she asks her father.

His face, petulant. 'She's not as nice as you think,' he says. 'I've just remembered something horrid about Great-aunt Alessandra.'

'What?'

'It's a secret.'

'What secret?'

'You must never tell.'

'I won't.'

'Not ever?'

'Not ever.'

He leans across the table in the train so that his face was close to hers. His green eyes, gloriously green, like wet dark seaweed in the rock pools.

Saskia's own eyes fly wide open in shock. Her father's mouth. She can see the shape of his nose. His broad handsome face, golden skin, white teeth. His tongue inside his mouth as he whispers the words to her.

'Great-aunt Alessandra is really a witch.'

Chapter 29

A witch!

Surging sickness. The awful tipping of her mind as she waits, watching her father's face, waiting for him to laugh, tell her it was a joke.

His expression does not change. 'I thought it was time you knew.' He nods his head. 'But it's a secret. No one else must know.'

Saskia cannot speak. A witch! Storybook characters leap alive in her head. The evil queen in 'Snow White'. The witch in the forest capturing Hansel and Gretel.

'You must never tell anyone.'

Saskia gives her head a tiny shake.

Her mother, returning from the toilet, looks from one to the other. 'What is it?

Her father winks. 'Our secret.'

And then she had been ill.

Her illness had nothing to do with Alessandra's house or the holiday. It had been months later, an outbreak of meningitis at school. She became desperately seriously ill. Her dreams, the nightmares of that terrible winter. Was

Alessandra like the witch in *Hansel and Gretel?* Did she cook children in her oven?

Saskia sees now the insides of fish, torn and bloody on the concrete floor of Peterhead Market. Alessandra at the kitchen table, filleting fish with a quick flick of her sharp knife.

'*Aunt Alessandra, why do we eat fish?*'

'*It is the way of things, little quine.*'

'*What things?*'

'*The very instance of life, the very tiniest creature in the sea is here for a purpose. We are in a cycle, part of the earth and the sea. The land was once sea and the sea is part of the clouds and the sky, an endless rhythm of life.*'

Alessandra smiles at Saskia. '*It's where we come from and where we go to. They say the herring follow the ancient rivers, the course laid out on the sea bed. When they return here, they are coming home.*'

Home. Safe. But some mothers and fathers reject their offspring, conspire together to abandon them. Decide their own interests are supreme. '*Babes in the Wood*', *that most terrifying of fairy tales. What could you do if you were the child? How could you protect yourself? Gretel had her brother. Hansel, his sister. Who did she, Saskia, have? No one. She wakes screaming, night after night. Living a waking nightmare. Alessandra, whom she loved, cannot be trusted.*

Now Saskia is sobbing in her mother's arms. '*I don't want to go back to Cliff House.*'

'*We won't go back.*' *Her mother holds her close.*

'*Promise?*'

'*I promise.*'

'*Not ever?*'

'Not ever.'

'Don't tell anyone it was me who said I don't want to go back.'

'I'll not tell.'

'No one?'

'No one. We'll never talk about it again.'

'WHY?' She was almost screaming down the phone at her father. 'Why did you say that awful horrible thing?'

'Saskia, calm down. I can hardly even remember us being on the train. It must have been a joke.'

'A joke! It terrified me. It made me not want to return as a child. Was it because she rejected you?

'What?'

'You told me how she rejected you and your mother. Sent you both away.'

'Saskia, I don't even recall saying that to you. If I did then it would have been meant as a joke. Honestly, I wouldn't have tried to scare you as much as that, but I do remember I was very annoyed with her.'

'Why?' Saskia asked her father more calmly now. 'Why would you even want to *think* of doing that?'

There was a silence.

'Was it the roof? You had hurt your hand.'

'Yes, yes. I had hurt my hand.'

'Something more?'

Saskia waited. She knew the reason. Alessandra had told her. But she wanted to hear her father say it himself.

'It was to do with a loan. I wanted to expand the business and she wouldn't lend me the money.'

'She doesn't *have* any money,' said Saskia. 'She lives very frugally.'

'All misers do,' said her father bitterly. 'I needed the money at that time and she knew it.'

'But she can't give you what she doesn't have.'

'She does. I know she does.'

'How can you possibly know that?'

There was a pause. 'Because she lent me money before. In fact she gave me the money to start the business . . . and,' he added casually, 'a few other bits and pieces, off and on. But it was you,' he went on with a rush, 'it was you that decided it for us. After you took ill you were so upset. That was when we decided not to go back.'

'I'd like to speak to Mum.'

'Darling' – her mother, usually so detached, distant, had words falling out of her mouth so fast Saskia could scarcely keep up with her – 'you screamed and screamed. You had horrible waking nightmares. We could not get you to talk sensibly. You kept saying that you did not want to go back to Cliff House, and finally I agreed that you would never go back, not ever. And you made me promise never to speak of the house or Alessandra again, and not to talk about this to your father. Darling, I would have promised you anything, anything. We thought you were going to die. Then we thought you were losing your mind. After I agreed never to mention it again you got better quite quickly, and I kept my promise, so each year we made up reasons not to go there.'

'My father told me a truly frightening lie about Aunt Alessandra.'

'But he wouldn't have done anything so deliberately

cruel as to keep you apart. Yes, he was deeply hurt as a child, and still gets upset about it. And you know how he is, about' – Saskia's mother hesitated – 'about blaming people for things. But he appreciates that Alessandra was sick in her mind for a while and should be excused her strange behaviour, and his mother, who was a kind woman, told me this too. She forgave Alessandra. In fact it was your grandmother Esther who asked us to visit Cliff House again. Before she died, she made us promise to take you to see Alessandra. We waited a bit, until you were nearly two years old, and then we went up there for a few days. You adored it, and Alessandra was besotted with you, so we kept going back. It was good for your father – the business stresses him and it made him take a break. And Alessandra and I got on well. I mean, she does have a certain obstinate way with her, but she has a fine mind, has read a lot, very knowledgeable—'

'And you painted.'

'Why yes, I did. I'd forgotten. In fact, some of my best stuff was from that time.'

'Why did I never see any of it around our house?'

'There's no mystery to that. Because it sold, darling. It was good art and people bought it. I might come up and join you for a week or so, give you a hand with Alessandra when she comes out of hospital. I could paint a bit more. Your father and I could do with some time off from each other. It might help . . . things.'

Saskia said nothing. Her mother had never before acknowledged that there might be a problem with her marriage.

Saskia knew what her parents had told her was the

truth, or as much as she would ever hear. They had probably wanted to go abroad anyway rather than spend time in the same place year after year. But it had been her, not them, who had not wanted to go back, all because of a stupid remark that her father had made on the train. Now he said he couldn't remember saying it. Maybe he couldn't. She would never know. At the time he was probably glad that it had happened, because he hadn't wanted her becoming too attached to the sea. He said he hadn't been seeking revenge, wasn't using it as a way to pay Alessandra back for not giving him more money. Saskia would never know if that was the complete truth either. Her father probably didn't know himself. He was so accustomed to bending the truth, adjusting things to suit himself, that even he wouldn't know.

'Hang on a minute.' Her mother had slowed down. 'Your father wants another word with you.'

'I'm sorry,' said Saskia's father. 'I'm really sorry if I upset you.'

A few minutes later Saskia hung up the phone. Her father had apologized. He had said 'sorry'. Properly and contritely, not a form of words or an 'excuse me' type of sorry, but a genuine apology, seeking forgiveness. '*I'm really sorry if I upset you.*' Saskia could not recall a single previous occasion where he had done that – taken responsibility for a mistake.

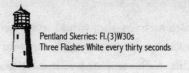

Pentland Skerries: Fl.(3)W30s
Three Flashes White every thirty seconds

Chapter 30

Saskia sat on the floor of the hall in the old house. The outline of the places where the furniture had once stood were clearly visible on the carpet: a chest of drawers on the stair landing, a table by the front door which might have held a bowl of fresh flowers.

Saskia got up and lit the storm lantern Alessandra kept in the kitchen. She went outside to the cellar under the stairs. The door creaked as she pushed it open and her shadow jumped before her. Saskia felt her heart-pace quicken but she was not afraid of the dark, she told herself, and she wanted to see what lay in the furthest reaches of this room.

She walked past the two bicycles, glancing at Alessandra's with its grotesquely shaped wheel. Her fingers lightly touched the harpoon propped against the wall. It must have belonged to Darach. What fears her great-aunt must have had when she knew Darach had gone whaling. Many boats did not return. Ships were trapped and crushed by the relentless arctic ice. The iceberg that sank the *Titanic* had come from south Greenland.

Against the wall stood the group of old herring barrels. Saskia spread her hand upon the cliff wall. The face of the rock was solid, but stuffed in behind the barrels was a pile of broken wood. Saskia set the lamp down on one of the barrels and bent to examine the pieces. They had been chopped into bits with an axe. She lifted what looked like spars from an old chair, and then saw that they were part of a child's cot. The wood was burnished mahogany and the light shone in its depths. Saskia knew that what she held in her hands was part of the cradle her father had slept in as a baby.

There were tears in her eyes as she came out of the cellar and closed the door behind her. She looked up at the great bulk of the house in front of her and then leaned her head right back and gazed at the night sky. Was that the Plough? The one the Americans called the Big Dipper? Big Dipper was a more obvious name – easy to see the outline of the ladle rather than the shape of an old-fashioned plough. One of the stars of that constellation pointed to the Pole Star.

Saskia raised the storm lantern high and turned to walk up the outside stairs. Twenty steps. How often had she done this as a child? She had expected all memories of her time here to come flooding back when the block of her childhood trauma had been removed, but they hadn't. She would have to wait. It would happen when it would happen.

She turned the handle of the attic door and stepped inside. Across the floor a scuttering sound. Mice? She held the lantern low. Eyes gleamed quickly among the herring nets and were gone. Rats? Saskia shivered. She hoped not. It could be one or more of any type of similar creature. She had told Ben about hearing sounds in the room above her head at night, and how, not knowing what it was, it made her slightly uneasy. He had suggested that it could be rabbits. He said they might have burrowed along the cliff or found another way in. They wouldn't stay in the attic but they might run about from time to time. Living mainly on the ground floor Alessandra wouldn't have heard these noises in the night.

The lantern cast shadows at odd angles throughout the attic. Saskia saw what she had previously thought was a bundle of blankets. In the light from the lantern the colour showed faded burgundy. She took an end of one with her hand and unfolded it. It was the curtains from the big front room of the house. Not torn down as her mother had said, but intact, and carefully folded in neat piles. Saskia picked up the shoe boxes containing the seashells and returned to the house.

First she went to her great-aunt's bureau. She did not feel that she was prying. She had to know. It didn't take her long to find what she was looking for, Alessandra did so little banking business. Saskia checked the dates of the dealers' receipts for the sale of house furniture against the cheque stubs in Alessandra's cheque book: the cheques made out to Saskia's father. They matched. Alessandra had sold the household goods to support Saskia's father's business.

As she ate dinner Saskia laid out her shell collection on the kitchen table. In the third box she found the one she was looking for. She walked through to the bookcase in the big room and searched for a book about shells. Saskia began to study the pages and pages of coloured plates. When she was collecting shells at six years old she had been too young to seek out information like this. Now she saw the entry she was looking for and another secret of Cliff House was revealed to her.

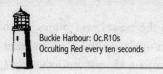

Chapter 31

Saskia put off starting her summer job and waited until her great-aunt had been home from hospital almost a week before she showed her the shell.

Alessandra picked it up and turned it over in her hand. She placed her thumb along the long curling lip. 'How beautiful are the creatures of the sea,' she murmured.

'The day that I found this shell beside the rock . . .' Saskia hesitated.

Alessandra met Saskia's eyes with a steady gaze, and Saskia saw how much improved her great-aunt was from her time in hospital. The strength had returned to her voice and she was eating most of the food Saskia prepared for her each day.

'I dreamed that I was crying that day,' said Saskia, 'but it wasn't me. It was you. When you saw the shell, I remember now, you picked me up. The taste of salt on my face *was* tears. But they were not mine, they were yours. You told me it was a British great whelk. I was only six years old so I believed you, and my parents did not even look at it properly. But no British shell is that colour or size. It is a Great Stair Shell from the seas of the Southern Ocean where Darach went whaling.'

Alessandra placed the shell on the table beside her bed. 'Darach found it on the shores of one of the islands of Japan and sent it to me. I used to carry it with me and it must have dropped from the pocket of my apron years ago. It upset me that day when I saw it. I recalled Darach, and how much I had lost. I think I lifted you up and hugged you so that you would not see me cry.'

'He sent you many gifts.' Saskia glanced at the double doors of the large wardrobe in Alessandra's bedroom. 'I'm sorry that I went into your private things. I was looking for clothes to bring to you in hospital and I unlocked your wardrobe.' She paused and, as Alessandra said nothing, went on, 'Why do you never wear any of those clothes? They are so beautiful.'

Alessandra clasped her hands together. Her fingers intertwined more loosely, Saskia noticed, rather than the stretched-tight clutching of the past.

'It was too painful and I had to be careful.'

'Careful of what?' asked Saskia. She looked at her great-aunt seriously. 'Alessandra, it would be better to talk about whatever it is that is worrying you.'

'You say this with such conviction that I am beginning to believe you.' Alessandra smiled and reached a hand out to stroke Saskia's cheek. 'We will talk, and I will tell you what happened to me when I was about your age.'

Saskia sat down by the side of the bed.

'It wasn't only my brother Rob who found love in Yarmouth town,' Alessandra began. 'One morning as I was at my work, topping the barrels with brine, I saw a young man looking at me. His name was Darach Keal.

211

He was from the Western Isles and his boat had docked into Yarmouth. Darach means an oak tree in Gaelic, and he was broad and strong like an oak, with eyes that had the colour of the ocean in them. There was a fair setting up on the town brae and he asked me if I would be there on Sunday, and I' – Alessandra gave a little laugh – 'I said, "I might be."

'That night I took my best dress from my kist and ironed it. Chris and May brushed out my hair and on Sunday we all went to the fair. He was waiting for me. I found out later that he'd been standing since dawn on the road to the fair. He asked me to walk with him, and we walked and talked, and we found that we liked the same things. Darach had the Gaelic. It was his first language. He had poetry in his head and the stories of the Gaels on his tongue, tales of the faery folk and water sprites, of kelpies and silkies. We walked all day, and then, in the evening, on the beach under the stars, he said he would come for me to my father's house.

'At the close of the season I went home. One winter's day his boat came into the harbour at Fhindhaven and he knocked on the door of Cliff House. My father was furious. He was not prepared to lose his housekeeper. But then he saw that I might leave with or without his permission, and he arranged with Darach that I could marry when he came back with enough money for us to set up house.

'So Darach agreed to go away and come back again when he had the money. He knew that he would not make such a sum in herring fishing so he went to the whaling. He tried Arctic whaling to begin with, and then went to North America.

'It was a weary winter for me. I began to knit him his own gansey to wear. I designed the pattern, chose the wools. It would be special for us. The moods of the sea and the brightness of the stars were in it. Moss stitch for the machair of the Western Isles and blackberry knots for the islands of his home. The colours were blue and brown, with yellow and grey.

'The next year Darach came back for me. My father said he had not made sufficient money to keep his daughter and would not let me speak to him alone. By that time Esther was with us, expecting Rob's child, and Rob was away to the herring fishing. She helped me slip away from the house one afternoon and I met Darach and we walked far from the town. He asked me to come away with him—'

Alessandra stopped in mid-sentence. Saskia, who had kept very quiet until now, said softly, 'Oh Alessandra. Now you wish you had gone with him.'

'But I couldn't,' Alessandra said with resignation. 'I did not tell you all of the conversation my brother Rob and I had the morning he left, and I walked with him part of the way to Fhindhaven.

'We stopped to say goodbye . . .

' "Alessandra," he said. "I worry about Esther and my unborn baby. If anything happens to me—"

' "Dinna say that!" I cried.

' "But if it did."

' "I'd take care of them," I said.

' "Our father frightens me at times."

' "No harm will come to them. I promise you."

'I told Darach about my promise to Rob, and Darach, being the man he was, agreed that I should stay in the house with Esther until Rob returned. As he left he said that when he next came back we would be married. This time, he said, he would go whaling to the South Seas. There was more money to be had there.'

'So you didn't break off your engagement to Darach?' said Saskia.

Alessandra shook her head. 'No,' she said, 'though I know that some people in the village thought I did. Darach sailed from Aberdeen and was months away by the time we knew that Rob had been killed. It was a difficult time for all of us. Darach wrote to me and said that he would go on to Japan and make enough money so that we could take Esther to live with us when he and I were married. Not long after that, I had to send Esther and her child away, so that she and your father would be safe. I could not bear to tell her of my suspicions about my own father.'

Alessandra looked at Saskia. 'It was a subject not spoken of then.'

'Even now,' said Saskia, 'victims of abuse say that they are too ashamed to speak out.'

'Although I was ashamed of my thoughts I knew I was not wrong,' said Alessandra. 'My father became incensed with rage when he found out that Esther was not return-ing. He took the baby crib and smashed it. I think that was to punish me. Eventually I put the remaining pieces at the back of the cellar. Even now I cannot bear to go inside and see the broken bits lying there.

'Then my father turned his gaze on me. I became

more and more disturbed by his way of following me around the house, always there, watching, waiting . . . I became very frightened. I wrote to Darach. I did not tell him everything, only that I wanted to leave my father's house at once. In the next parcel that Neil Buchan smuggled to me, Darach sent money. I prepared myself to leave.

'But my father knew I was being secretive, and searched through my things. He found the money. He took it. He shut me in my room and said he would deal with me later, that there would be no escape for me. But early that night I climbed down from the window, left the house and began to walk south, away from Fhindhaven. I had only gone a few hundred yards when I heard steps on the road behind me.

'He was pursuing me.

'I left the road and ran onto the cliff path. He caught up with me above the rocks at the headland. He ordered me to come home. I refused. He tried to pull me back. He was tearing at my clothes. We struggled. With great force I pushed him away.'

Alessandra stopped speaking, her eyes huge and dark in her face.

'Before my eyes he disappeared.'

'He fell from the cliff?' Saskia whispered.

Alessandra put her hands over her face.

Saskia's heart trembled within her. 'He fell from the cliff,' she repeated.

'I didn't know what to do,' said Alessandra. 'The water was high. I hoped he'd missed the rocks. I ran back to the house and tried to take our lobster boat out. The tide was running. The boat spun away from me. I ran to the Buchans' house. Only Neil was at home. He cycled to the village and they launched the lifeboat. They found the boat run aground under the headland. Everyone thought my father had been in the boat when it was driven onto the rocks. It was many weeks later that his body was washed up further down the coast. No one thought it was anything other than a fishing accident. I decided to let them think that. I began to think if I told the truth I would be charged with murder.' Alessandra paused. 'Sometimes I still believe that that could happen.'

'No!' said Saskia. 'It was an accident.'

'It is well known that I rebelled against him. If there is no evidence, sometimes people think the worst.'

'That's why you have this fear of being taken away!'

'The fear is real. My father fell to his death in nineteen fifty-one and in nineteen fifty-two a woman was hung for murder in England.'

Saskia put her hand to her throat.

'I live with the fear,' said Alessandra. 'And the guilt.'

'It is not your fault.' Saskia said in a low voice. 'He slipped and fell to his death.'

'I pushed him away from me.'

Saskia shook her head. 'You were defending yourself.'

'When he tried to take me home, I should not have resisted,' said Alessandra. 'I was brought up to believe that a child owed obedience to a parent.'

Surely not if the parent is abusing their child, Saskia thought. But she looked at Alessandra's face and didn't say anything.

'I waited for Darach,' said Alessandra. 'I thought,

Darach will come, and I will see everything more clearly. Every morning and evening I went to the top room and looked out to sea and imagined I could see the boat that was bringing him home to me. But then word came that his ship had foundered and all the crew were drowned. Another whaling ship picked up the bodies floating in the sea and took them to the nearest port.

'He is buried on an island somewhere in the South Seas.'

Saskia's eyes were full of tears.

Alessandra said, 'I don't mean to upset you.'

'What about you?' asked Saskia. 'You must stop if telling me all this is too distressing for you.'

'There are days when sadness overwhelms me,' said Alessandra, 'but it is not such a turbulent grief as it was once.' She looked out of the window. 'I am glad that he is on an island. I like to think of him sleeping there, wrapped in the gansey that I knitted.'

Kinnaird Head: Fl.W5s
Flashing White every five seconds

Chapter 32

Saskia too looked out of the window. The mottled face of a grey moon rode low in the sky. To the southwest, yellow licks of sky and violet cloud trails showed an early summer sunset.

'I used to wake some mornings and think I dreamed all of it,' said Alessandra.

'And there was no one at all you could talk to?' asked Saskia.

'I did not want to put my burden onto anyone else and there was a great stigma about mental illness in those days,' Alessandra went on. 'The village already gossiped about me. How cruel I had been to tell Esther to leave. I also heard them saying that I'd sent Darach away because I wanted a man with more money than he had. I was very isolated. Chris and May married fishermen from other parts and left Fhindhaven. Chris was in the Orkneys, May lived in South Shields. There was no one to confide in. Neil was only a boy.'

'Is that when you became ill?'

'Yes. After my father's funeral I started to confuse the days of the week, and then the distinction between sunrise and sunset began to blur. I had no thought of what I did or ate or wore. I dressed in clothes of wild colours that did not match. Although some people did try to help me, I became the strange woman of the village. Children called names after me.

'Then my mind slipped into a place I did not know. I would wake and be on the beach by the rocks or the stairs to the attic, anywhere, but not in the house. In my dreams I saw their faces – Rob, my father, Darach. In the night they walked beside me. I ranged between hysteria and despair. I stood on the cliff and thought of casting myself off.

'I thought I must tell someone, anyone, that I had murdered my father. I went to the police station in Peterhead. I stood outside in the street. I thought about what they might do to me if I confessed to murder. I stood there so long that when nightfall came I did not know my name.

'I turned round and walked back to Cliff House.

'The next day when I woke up I knew that I did not want to hang. And the day I knew that I did not want to hang was the day I knew that I wanted to live. I saw that I needed help. I took the bus to Aberdeen and went to a hospital and asked to be taken in.'

'How brave you were to do that,' said Saskia. 'I cannot imagine what it was like.'

'It was not the most cheerful place to be,' said Alessandra. 'Treatment of mental illness at that time could be very harsh. Yet individual nurses were kind, and one doctor was very practical. After a space of time he told me I must go home. I did not want to. The routine and order supported me. It meant I needed to think less. I see now that he believed I was becoming institution-alized, but it was very difficult for me to adjust to the world again. Even now I struggle to be at ease in company.

'So I came back to Cliff House. I had to be careful, how I ate, how I spoke, and with my choice of clothes. I had to re-learn how to behave.

'I found that if I wore black or grey I made fewer mis-takes. This also made it much easier to dress each day. It didn't matter what you chose – it would never clash or look wrong.'

Saskia thought of the silk dresses, the colourful jackets in Alessandra's wardrobe.

'I still see a psychiatrist every few months. And I take pills when the doctor tells me to. The tablets help sedate me, but mostly they have the effect of slowing my physical reactions. How do you switch off emotion? I feel things *here*' – Alessandra put her hand to heart – 'too deeply. That first day when you arrived and you said my name, *Alessandra*, it struck at my heart. You called me "Aunt Alessandra". No one in our family had said my name for many years. Then you walked down my path and spoke my name . . . Alessandra.

'*Alessandra.*

'Darach's way of saying my name was quite beautiful.'

"Alessandra, my Alessandra
I dream of you tonight
Across the dark sky the stars speak to me
The wind is in the trees, the leaves whisper your name.

I awaken and I call out
Alessandra."'

Alessandra began to weep quietly and Saskia again felt tears on her own cheeks. She stood up. 'I'll make some tea,' she said.

Alessandra stretched out her hand. 'No, no, sit down. I will finish.'

'I'm worried that it is taking too much out of you,' said Saskia. 'You should rest.'

'The story is nearly finished and as it ends with you then you should hear it.'

Saskia sat back down upon the bed.

'For many years I was in and out of hospital but slowly I began to heal. Esther brought you here as a newborn baby, and then I think, before she died, she made your father promise to bring you to visit me. When your father came the first time to see me he told me he wanted to start his own business. In exchange for all my father's money he signed the house to me legally. He would probably have had some claim on it through Rob, so I was glad to have the security, and he was glad to have the independence that the money gave him. When the lawyer telephoned to say the house was totally mine I sat in the big room all day until the light left the sky, and land and sea became one. Then I switched on the lamps. I always remember Rob saying that he looked to the house as his boat made for port at the end of the season. That night I took down all the curtains. I have never replaced them.

'For five or six years you visited in the summer, and

you were so young and innocent that you saw nothing strange in my manner. I could talk quite naturally to you. From when you were very small you would ask me to take you to the village for sweets or ice cream and I could not refuse you. You chattered to everyone you met, so it made it easier for me to talk to others.'

'It must have been an awful disappointment when we stopped coming,' said Saskia with a sense of discomfort.

'It was. Yet the good you had done stayed with me. I would not have been able to do work for the Heritage Centre had I not renewed my contact with people and the village.'

Saskia was reluctant to tell Alessandra of her father's joke that had led to her trauma and the reason she had never returned to Cliff House as a child. To do so would only make it harder for her father and Alessandra to resume their relationship. 'The other night I remembered something that happened on the train on the way home from our last visit here as a family,' she began awkwardly. 'I got a fright . . . and then it was mixed up with me being ill. I think that was why I said I didn't want to visit you again. I'm so sorry that happened.'

Alessandra reached out and took Saskia's hand. 'It doesn't matter,' she said softly. 'Dinna fret, little quine.'

Chapter 33

From the clifftop path Saskia could see Alessandra walking on the beach.

Supported with two sticks, her great-aunt was doing the daily exercise routine suggested by the hospital. Neil Buchan was walking with her. Patient Neil. Saying little, but knowing much. Had he guessed the truth about the death of Alessandra's father? Alessandra had run to his house for help on that dreadful night. He must have seen that her clothes were torn. He would have said nothing for fear of shaming her, but had remained faithful over the years, supporting her when she needed it. Waiting for her to love him.

Saskia was pleased with her own scheme to foster this romance. She had persuaded Alessandra to allow Neil to help her down to, and up from, the beach each morning. She had threatened not to begin the summer job at the Research Station today unless Alessandra agreed. Alessandra was dressed, as always, in dark trousers and cardigan. But she was wearing a scarf that Saskia had given her. A bright blue scarf.

Saskia turned away and began to walk towards

Fhindhaven. Ben had warned her about how boring she might find the research work, but she'd already lost some time by nursing Alessandra after her accident and was now eager to begin. Only by doing the work would she find out if her interest in the sea extended to making a career for herself in some marine-related subject. And if she did, then it would not just be because she had met Ben.

Saskia found that she was smiling when she thought of Ben. The more time she spent with him and got to know him, the more she liked him. Which was certainly a change for her. The opposite usually happened with any boy she fell for. Alan, who had been a major feature in her last year at school, had come with her on the trip to Nepal. Close contact over the ensuing weeks had soured that relationship very quickly. With Ben it was different. Each new aspect of his character was appealing, like his way of listening quietly when someone else was speaking, his particular attention to her great-aunt. It was not just that Ben took the trouble to visit Alessandra, it was the manner of his attention. He seldom brought presents like flowers or sweets. His kindness took the form of time, talking with Alessandra, discussing fishing and the sea. And he was also fun to be with, thought Saskia. It would be interesting to see what her parents, her father, would make of him.

Her parents . . . She tried to think of them objectively. Why did they both cling to her when they seldom listened to her, or talked about her interests? She supposed that their self-centredness was one of their faults and she had to accept, as a grown-up, that her parents had faults.

She could, did, still love them, although at the moment she was finding it difficult. She now believed that they wanted her to remain close to home so that she could be a reason for them to stay together. And in the past she always fell in with her father's wishes because she liked to please him, and the emotional fall-out from not doing so was too much for her to cope with. But she was finished with that. She would no longer be Daddy's 'best girl' and automatically take the university course that he had chosen for her. She'd ask Ailsa at the Fhindhaven Marine Research Station for career information. She might apply to Aberdeen or St Andrews University and do marine biology. Ben's conviction was that human ingenuity would be our undoing if we allowed it to destroy the natural cycles of the planet. The waters round Britain, which had been the breeding grounds of a thousand species for a million years, were being ransacked. The next twenty years or so would see the results of the European regulations. Ben and his colleagues, and the fisherfolk, needed help and support to protect the fish if there were going to be fish left by the time of the new century.

Her parents would have to deal with their life without her. More than likely her father wouldn't support her if she moved away, and it came to Saskia why her mother stayed with her father. It was for the same underlying reason that she herself had caved in over her career choice. It had been the easiest thing to do. If you made decisions for yourself then you had to take full responsibility for them, and that was a more challenging path to follow. But there would be cafés or pubs in Aberdeen or

St Andrews where she could get work and earn some money. She'd grind out her own lens through which she viewed the world. She loved both her parents but she could no longer tailor her life to suit their aspirations. It would be difficult to disentangle herself. Like shipwrecked Gulliver, tied down by each individual hair, she must loosen herself strand by strand.

Saskia remembered a puzzle her class had been given in maths. They were shown a diagram – a box containing a series of lines at different angles. The exercise had been to extend the lines and connect them in order to make as many triangles as possible. They had all failed to achieve the maximum number. 'You've all got blinkers on,' the maths teacher had laughed as she had drawn the solution on the board, extending the lines through the frame of the box. 'You are bound by regulation and inert thought. I didn't say that you couldn't extend a line beyond the box. Think outside the frame,' she urged. 'One day you may have to.'

Now Saskia's frame was going to be removed, and she was the one who was going to do it. But she would be by the sea.

Where she belonged.

Their cycle complete, the shoals prepare to move on. Guided by the ocean itself they start to make their way out to deeper water, leaving the spawning grounds rich with new life . . .

AUTHOR'S NOTE

During the writing of *Saskia's Journey* the future
of the European fisheries reached a new level
of crisis. Confronted with insensitive legislation
coastal communities face annihilation, while
aggressive and industrial fishing threatens
the balance of life on our planet.

In this novel the sea has a voice –
we should listen.

ABOUT THE AUTHOR

'An outstanding writer… simply superb'
Independent

THERESA BRESLIN is a librarian and writer
who lives in a village in Central Scotland.
Nearby are lots of castles, ancient burial grounds
and the Roman Wall, all of which helped fuel an
active imagination as a child, further developed
by a real love of reading. Her writing combines
a powerful sense of drama with memorable
characters and superb storytelling.

Her first book, *Simon's Challenge*, won the Young
Book Trust's Fidler Award for new writers and, since
then, her books have appeared regularly on many
children's book award shortlists. She was awarded
the Carnegie Medal for *Whispers in the Graveyard*.
Her work has also been filmed for television and
dramatised on radio, and she was recently awarded
lifelong Honorary Membership of the Scottish
Library Association for distinguished services to
Children's Literature and Librarianship.

THERESA BRESLIN

Remembrance

'They will never forget . . . Nor will anyone
who picks up this novel' *Writers' News*

**Summer 1915, and the sound of the guns at the Western
Front can be heard across the Channel in England.**

**Throughout Britain, local regiments are recruiting
for Kitchener's Army. And in the village of
Stratharden, the Great War is to alter irrevocably
the course of five young lives . . .**

**An epic novel from award-winning
author Theresa Breslin.**

'Breslin brilliantly weaves the themes of emancipation,
class, love, propaganda and the machinations of war
into the story of how these young lives are changed with
a light touch that belies the seriousness of the subject.
A Pat Barker for young readers' *Financial Times*

'Breslin's light touch and beautiful prose give the
harrowing sights and sounds of the war a much
more human feel . . . a novel that will stay
with me for a long time' *The Bookseller*

'A truly epic feel . . . already *Remembrance* is being
hailed as Breslin's best book yet' *Glasgow Herald*

0552 547387